LUCKY DAYS

LUCKY BREAK SERIES

HOPE MALONE

BAD BIRDS
Squabbling Sparrows Press

ONE

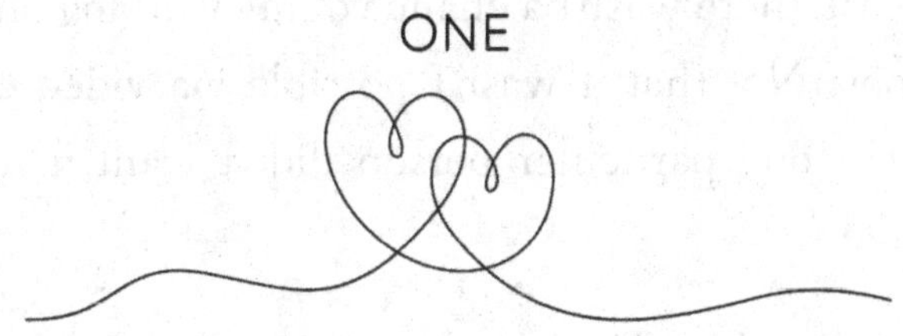

KELLY

On glancing away from my computer screen to give my eyes a rest, I barely notice the killer view. It's receded into the background, like many other things.

It hadn't always been this way. On first finding myself stranded at the family vacation home when the world imploded, I was in hog heaven. There were worse places to be stuck for a couple of weeks.

After a month, the novelty was gone. I missed the bustle of the agency. Of interacting with my colleagues and being automatically included in any projects for the agency's star clients.

That privilege ended so quickly that it was a wonder I hadn't suffered from whiplash. Stuck all the way up the coast, there wasn't a chance of my working on the big jobs. Not that it wasn't possible via video calls, but that one particular person didn't want it to be possible.

Jason Ralph! The agency's Aussie Executive Creative Director who's creative in title only. I'd lost count of the number of times he'd taken the credit for my concepts, claiming them as his own.

When it looked like the lockdown was going to last awhile, I'd asked if he could send me my computer so I could carry on remotely. But, according to him, someone else was now using it.

Meanwhile, I had to get along as best I could on the fully spec'd laptop they'd given me and that I'd only packed at the last minute. There was always a chance I'd have to alter a campaign when I was on vacation.

While it was a great laptop, it wasn't up to the challenge of working on large projects from scratch. I knew what Jason was up to, because I wouldn't be the first person who'd had no option other than to resign thanks to his toxic management style.

I swear he could give that Aussie newspaper guy a run for his money with that. There's a term for what Jason was doing. Constructive termination. And, yes, it was illegal and something I could fight in court.

Whether I would, I still wasn't sure. As was often the case, the target wouldn't have the fight left to take it further. To delay the inevitable, I'd invested in a decent computer of my own. I was then surprised to find I liked it even better than the one the agency deemed good enough for me. Mine was definitely faster.

When lock-down showed no sign of ending, I'd called the neighbor who was watering my plants, and asked her to pack up some clothes for me. I'd also told her to clear out my fridge and to keep any champagne she found for her troubles.

She was more than willing to help after that.

I figured when lock-down was over, I'd move back to LA and get on with life. Boy, was I ever wrong.

Jason had other ideas, and I wasn't the only one caught up in his grandiose reorganization. It hadn't taken the top brass at the agency long to work out they could save money by having us work from home. It also allowed them to sub-let two of the three floors in the high rise.

As to the floor left populated? That'd be the one with all the beautiful people on staff, at least when it came to the female employees. These days, only the young blonde intern from my old team still graces the halls of MC&S.

The other way Jason had made it impossible for me to move back was by reducing my income, citing the pandemic as the reason. More likely, he wanted to bring on more young blonde interns to further bolster his flagging ego.

It was yet another nail in the constructive dismissal coffin, and yet I held on, my stubborn streak coming to the fore. Bitter? Me?

I'd always known Jason hated my not being stick-thin and magazine-ready as other women on staff were. There was no missing the way his lip would curl when I'd walk into his office to present my concepts. There was no missing him belittling my concepts, even though we both knew they were solid.

Just how solid always came to light when the client opted for them over anything Jason cobbled together. And yep, it was then Jason would claim my ideas as his own. I'd have loved him to try it when I was in the room, but he'd made sure I never was.

My phone ringing has me back to the present, rather than at the agency in LA.

"Hey, mom. How's it going?"

As always, my mom sounds surprised by my question. It's as though I've phoned her, and not the reverse.

"Oh, oh, it's, ah. It's going well. Listen darling, remember how we've been talking about renovating Sand 'O' Sun?"

I do, with my parents discussing updating the aptly named Sanderson vacation home for as long as I could remember. This has me answering, as I always do. "You have, and it's long overdue."

However, while I've stuck to the script on this, mom has other ideas.

"Thanks for understanding. The builders will be there tomorrow." Distracted as always, she then tells someone in the background she'll be with them in a jiffy.

This gives me a second or two to process her bombshell. However, it's nowhere long enough to digest the ramifications.

"Listen, sweetie. I have to go. I'm last to tee off. Your father's booked Lucky Break Construction. You know the one?"

Without giving me time to confirm either way, she presses on. "Yes, yes. The company, young Ethan Hunter from Eagle's Nest, started up. Better go, the girls are getting itchy. Love you."

And with that she's gone, leaving me to wonder what sort of renovation she and my dad have decided on. They've discussed everything over the years. From touching up the paint and replacing the windows, to demolition and starting over.

I sure hope it's not the latter. Apart from loving the ramshackle nature of the place, it would involve me moving out. I can't handle this on top of everything else.

A quick call to my dad allays some of my fears. Updating the kitchen and opening the house to the garden I can live with. It won't be fun, but if I shut myself in the front bedroom that I've set up as my office and wear my noise-canceling headphones, I should be okay.

I'm thinking this right until I see two trucks pull up outside the following day. Nothing exciting there. However, when two of the hottest men I've seen outside of a photo shoot clamber out of the vehicles, I have to wonder.

While both men are gorgeous, it's the slightly shorter man who catches my eye. There's something about him that has my mind crowded with hammering, and it's got nothing to do with construction.

ZAC

On pulling up behind Tyler Pierce at the Sanderson place, I'm pissed. I had a chance with Lily, the owner of the place we'd been helping flip. I just know it.

It's always been this way. Well, at least from high school when I'd shot up to my current six-foot-one. And yet, I'm a short-ass next to Tyler and the others on the crew. Sheesh, the Kendrick brothers are massive, with Josh being a complete unit.

Lucky for me is the woman who answers Tyler's knock is just the right height, and damn if I don't love those curves. Although, they aren't what hit me hardest.

That would be her dark brown eyes and that curly explosion of tiger striped brown hair. Both hint at hidden depths and a wild side. One I'll be happy to plumb, or tame, or maybe even both?

While Tyler outlines how the job will progress, I keep my eyes on Kelly Sanderson as she's introduced herself. Odd, but after staring at me long enough for me to smile and wink, she's ignored me.

I'm left feeling invisible, which annoys me more than it should. I'm used to women fawning over me, not cutting me dead like this. Still, I'm always willing to take on a challenge. Especially one as cute as this.

It's when she invites Tyler inside and shuts the door in my face that I see it mightn't be that easy. What have I done to have her pulling that stunt?

I'm working alongside Tyler, so wouldn't it make more sense for me to be inside for the briefing? Her shutting me out like this has me wondering if she's worth the trouble. That stuck up...

As the days' progress, I decide I don't like Kelly Sanderson, with her clearly hating Coogan's Break. Sure, she's gorgeous, but from the little I see or hear of her, she's your typical city girl.

Uninterested in the beauty of Coogan's and our laid-back lifestyle, she comes across as only killing time until she can return to the city.

Despite all this, she still does it for me. Maybe her being unavailable has her doing it for me in a BIG way. As with our first day on site, she's continued to ignore me.

My preoccupation was obvious enough that even the grunts taken on to help with demo and general labor had noticed it.

For a start, Tyler had even laughed about it. Now he's getting annoyed, using every excuse he can to have me leave the site to collect supplies.

"Zac, you need to give it a rest. If Ethan sees you drooling over the client like that, he'll fire your ass."

There's no need to ask him what he's talking about. Ethan, our boss, while easy going, has one rule with clients. And that's that the only screwing allowed on site is the type that involves power tools.

For all the notice that some of the crew take. Case in point being Brad, who's now living with a jewelry designer whose studio Lucky Break had built.

With Tyler off site, the grunts decide it's safe to rib me about my obsession and my lack of results. It's enough to have me hammering harder than I need to in order to drown them out.

Far better, I take my frustrations out on a piece of wood. Despite coming close to obliterating the nail I'm working on; I still hear the loud crash from inside the house.

My head jerks up, and I'm surprised to see Kelly standing at the kitchen window, her face a mask of shock. I drop my hammer and am on my way to the backdoor in a flash, because something spooked her.

A brief knock and I open the door, although only far enough that I can ask if she's okay. Her response being gibberish, I risk walking inside. It's only on rounding the corner and entering the kitchen that I see the chaos.

As is common with these older places, our hammering away has highlighted a few problems. Here, it's one of the upper kitchen cabinets coming away, leaving an unpainted patch behind on the wall.

The solid wood cabinet now lies on the floor next to Kelly, its contents strewn from one end of the kitchen to the other. As quick as I've been to take stock of the chaos, I'm next to her in a heartbeat. I then guide her to put the French press of hot coffee down on the counter.

The last thing she needs is third-degree burns when she drops it, as she is likely ready to do.

"Are you okay?"

While she starts off nodding, this soon changes to a shake, shock clear in her eyes. With her trembling intensifying by the second, I wrap my arms around her.

Despite my attraction, the move is one of comfort. That cabinet must have missed her by a whisker. If it had connected, we'd now be on our way to the emergency room, or waiting for the paramedics with a backboard.

Instead, I steer her away from the other cabinets, and over to the dining nook. Once seated, I return and grab the French press of coffee, along with the mug that had been next to it.

Rather than sit down, I pour her a coffee and step back. While I want to stay and comfort her, I can't. I've seen something out of the corner of my eye that needs attention more than this stunning woman.

The next cabinet along is also hanging on by a thread, something that has me making quick work of emptying the contents onto the counter.

A gentle tug on the empty cabinet, and it comes away from the wall, with me then lowering it to the floor. She was lucky not to be flattened after the recent earthquakes.

It doesn't take long to see the other cabinets are also an accident waiting to happen. I don't bother asking for permission, instead emptying them and ripping them off the walls. It's a good thing we're renovating the kitchen, because it was only a matter of time before someone got taken out by a falling cabinet.

A quick gander at Kelly, her coffee still untouched, and I have to wonder who, or what, hurt her in the past? Despite her stonewalling me, her coming close to being brained by that cabinet had her walls coming down.

And even though it'd missed her, there'd been plenty of hurt showing in those dark brown eyes.

TWO

KELLY

As I sit staring at my cooling coffee, I'm having trouble processing just how close I'd come to being hit by that cabinet. It was my fault. I shouldn't have slammed the door as hard as I had.

But I was furious after reading Jason's latest email. The one telling me Deb, my copywriting partner, had resigned. It had to have been sudden, as we'd only caught up late yesterday. I need to ring her and find out what happened, but I can't, not when I'm still dealing with the other bad news in the email.

As an art director on their own, I have little value in the agency and it's for this reason I'm being demoted to general agency design work. Bye-bye big-ticket creative campaigns for me. Without a copywriter, I'm adrift, without purpose.

That, that ... As my mom often said, ladies don't cuss, but boy Jason deserved a few choice words. That ... that... jerk.

With Deb gone, I'm not sure how much longer I can hold out, because in tandem with my demotion, came yet another pay cut. Even knowing what Jason is up to doesn't make it easier to swallow.

It's only a matter of time before I'm forced to search for another position. That's if I can, with no agency interested in half a creative team. The sooner I catch up with Deb, the better.

If we can apply for a job as a team, then we stand a chance of securing something. Without that, I'm trapped.

After pushing my coffee to one side, I slump forward, my forehead pressed against the cool tabletop. Life shouldn't be this hard, should it? I'd graduated at the top of my class, and had the awards to prove I was competent at my job.

So why was I being forced out by that glorified crocodile hunter?

There's nothing I can do to stop a snort of amusement at thoughts of Jason wrestling with one of those scaly beasts. The only way he'd win would be by boring the reptile to death with one of his cruddy campaigns.

I'm still hunched over when something is placed on the table next to me. On tipping my head to the side, I see it's a plate with two chocolate chip cookies. This is weird. I know there aren't any in the house. If there were, I'd have used them to self-medicate by now.

"You eat those while I make a fresh coffee." Zac pushes the plate even closer, before saying, "You need sugar after a shock like that."

It's enough to have me straightening, to stare at him. I soon enough regret it when I'm the target of yet another of those cocky grins. Honestly, do women fall for that crap?

He's like so many men I've worked with in advertising that I can't stop myself from rolling my eyes. It's enough to have his smile faltering before he tips his head toward the plate.

"Eat."

Following this order, he grabs my still full cup of coffee and the French press and takes them over to the sink. Only now do I notice the surrounding chaos. Instead of there being one upper cabinet on the kitchen floor, all of them are.

Piled up like Stonehenge, with the microwave perched atop, their contents stacked high on every available surface.

"What the heck!?"

How on earth did I miss him dismantling the kitchen?

"Tyler said you wouldn't start with the kitchen for a week or two."

"That was before I saw the cabinets were held in place with glue and good wishes."

After a lot of bustling about, during which I admit he's got a body to die for, or even under, he puts a fresh coffee in front of me. He follows this up by yet again, instructing me to eat. Then, without another word, he leaves.

My first mouthful of cookie and I'm not concentrating, although this soon changes. There isn't a chance I'd miss cookies as delicious as these in the cupboards. I can smell chocolate at twenty paces.

The other thing that stops me from taking another bite is that if I didn't know better, I'd think they were homemade.

Now I'm even angrier at Zac for giving me all those cocky smiles. Despite them being as fake as the guy himself, my response to his comforting hug has been anything but.

After being jammed up against his muscled chest, my libido has been knocked about enough that it may as well have been taken out by a kitchen cabinet.

Another nibble of cookie and I'm more convinced than ever that he's gotta be married or living with someone. With my nerves and libido still on a knife's edge, I'm not sure which option upset me more.

Thankfully, I've got one-and-a-half cookies to help with the shock.

Now I'm torn. Do I stay in the kitchen and try to make sense of everything? Or, do I start work on the

Burt's Pet Food web tile Jason wants me to complete in my new role as agency lackey?

Then I decide I won't give him the satisfaction of my missing the deadline, even though it's tight because he wants it so.

"It is on, you Aussie reptile!"

I'm not sure if it's the sugar talking, but I'm soon back in front of my computer, determined to create the best pet food ad known to humankind. Or should that be dog kind?

The trick will be Jason not bothering to check the concept before he forwards it to the client. As lazy as he is, chances are he won't even open the attachment before sending it on. It's also a given he'll remove any reference to my email when he does so.

If the client loves the concept, by then it'll be too late for him to backtrack. For me to rework the agency's DRAFT watermark so that it includes my name will be easy.

While I've let my personal website fall by the wayside since working for MC&S, come tomorrow morning, it will carry a full complement of my work in recent years.

You never knew when a client would want to learn more about you. This was especially true when I knew Jason wouldn't be forthcoming.

As immersed as I am in updating my website, I freak out when someone knocks on the window right next to me. On my gaze flying in that direction, I note two things. It's Zac, and it's pitch-black outside.

How did it get so late? The last thing I remember was a bathroom break mid-afternoon, at which time I realized I hadn't had lunch. After a quick check of the kitchen, I'd put it in the too-hard basket.

My plan had been, after sending the web tile design to Jason, I'd head into town and grab some frozen meals. Enough to last me until the kitchen is rebuilt.

It's then I notice Zac is holding a plastic carry bag with a familiar logo on the side, and all thoughts of heat-and-eat flee. Something nuked in the microwave atop Stonehenge falls short compared to anything from the Thai Palace. The best takeaway in Coogan's Break.

On my opening the front door, he's waiting for me.

"I felt so bad about demolishing your kitchen. I wanted to make up for it." He nods toward the front of the house. "When I saw you were still working, I figured you might not have eaten yet."

ZAC

I'm confident until I knock on the window next to Kelly. I'm helping her out, that's all. Then a little voice whispers, "Yeah, sure you are."

And while I could fool others into thinking I'm turning a good deed; I can't fool myself. Of course, I've got an ulterior motive. I always do. I've always got my eye on the prize. This time, it's Kelly Sanderson.

All that changes the minute she answers the front door and I deliver my rehearsed lines. She's not buying it, at least in so far as my motive goes, her expression confirming it.

Once again, she's got me on the back foot, a stance I'm unfamiliar with. I'm ready to hand her the food and do a runner, when she again surprises me.

"That's so thoughtful of you." While polite, her words are also non-committal, leaving me unsure of where I stand, apart from on the bottom step. All that changes when she adds. "Why don't you come in? It looks as though you've bought enough for two."

Why is it she can see right through me? The lady at the Thai Palace may as well have written 'HOPING TO GET LAID' on the side of the bag, rather than 'ZAC'. It's clear, at least to me, that this is what Kelly has read into an order that's too big for one person.

"Thanks, but you're busy. I'll be on my way." The words are out before I've had time to craft them. To work on another angle.

Now it looks as though I've surprised her. However, rather than reach out and take the proffered bag, she instead huffs out in annoyance. Despite this, she steps to the side in silent invitation.

It's one I'm having second thoughts about accepting. On dinner dates with gorgeous women, I'm used to being welcomed with open arms. I don't need her pity. I've still not made a move, or even moved, when she speaks.

"Are you married or living with someone?" As abrupt as her question has been, I'm as fast to shake my head. It's all I can do not to spit out, "Hell, no!"

"Good, in that case, come on in. I need a second opinion on something. But let's eat first."

While not a gracious invitation, her request is intriguing. How can a guy with my skill set help someone like her? Isn't she a flash city designer, or something?

Deciding there's only one way to find out, I walk inside, heading toward the kitchen. Despite my having left it like a bombsite, it's there we'll find plates and cutlery.

And also glasses for water. If I'd turned up with beers or a bottle of wine, my true purpose would have been all too obvious. I needn't have worried, given how quickly she'd spotted my ruse.

When I flick on the lights, I'm surprised to find everything as it had been when I'd left earlier. The only plate on the counter is the one I'd used to give her the cookies I'd grabbed at the bakery.

After clearing a spot on the counter, I drop the bag and turn to her. "Did you even have lunch?"

She stops in her riffling through the teetering piles of plates and turns to me. "Didn't have time. I'm on, or I was on, deadline." There's then no missing the smug grin she indulges in, with her even snorting out in laughter.

She then mutters something about Crocodile Dundee, all while grabbing two large bowls and forks and spoons. I'm glad she hasn't opted for chopsticks because I always end up wearing my dinner when I try to wrangle those.

And while I might not stand a chance with Kelly, I don't want to appear the fool in front of her, either. It's obvious she already thinks I'm a hick, and I guess I am compared to the city types she'd be used to dating.

Dating? Yeah, in your dreams, bro.

That goal out of the way, my appetite returns with a vengeance. A loud rumble from my stomach is enough to have me taking the aluminum containers out of the plastic bag and removing their lids.

Rather than carry everything over to the table in the dining nook and have oil and sauce go everywhere, we serve up at the counter.

My first mouthful of green chicken curry, and I'm regretting my decision not to bring beers. Mild my ass.

Likewise, Kelly is busy fanning her mouth, beads of perspiration further drawing my attention to her lush lips. Rather than stay seated, she jumps up, but instead of getting us glasses of water as I've expected, she opens the fridge.

A moment later and she passes me an opened bottle of beer, her hand brushing against mine, with a jolt of electricity passing between us.

Not bothering to clink my beer against hers, I draw on it, welcoming the cooling benefits of the drink both on my mouth and my mounting arousal. I've drained half the beer before I put it down next to my bowl, my hands shaking with the effort of keeping them to myself.

While I might say, "Sorry, I asked for mild," there's nothing mild about my attraction to Kelly. I suspect I'm not alone in this. When her gaze locks with mine, her pupils dilate, giving her eyes a dark intensity.

It's one that hints at depths as fiery as anything the Thai Palace have on their menu. However, the next time I glance up, it's as if I'm sitting opposite a different woman, one who doesn't find me attractive in the least.

.   .   .

It's because of this, that I keep to neutral topics, like the renovation. Much as I want to get to know Kelly 'better', she's a spikey one. If I push it, she'll send me packing.

The only thing that doesn't cool off is the curry, with us on our second beer apiece before we finish. I've gotta admit to having quite the buzz after having drunk them, one after the other.

It's no wonder Tyler and the other guys call me a lightweight in that department.

"Now, what was it you wanted my opinion on?" While images of her in a body-con dress crowd my mind, I doubt this is what she wants my help with.

It takes a second for her to work out what I'm talking about. When she does, she's on her feet as fast as she had been when in search of beer.

"Come on through to my office." She's then off without waiting for me to follow.

On walking into her office, and seeing what she's been working on, there's nothing I can do to stop my laughter. Not at her design, but the content.

"Oh, that's brilliant!"

"You get it?"

I'm busy nodding before I voice my confirmation. "Are you kidding? Of course, I get it and it's funny as hell. Jeez, I'd be tempted to buy their dog roll, and I don't even own a dog!"

It's at this point I'm rewarded by Kelly smiling at me.

And then I have to ruin it all by winking at her. I hadn't meant to, but I'm like Pavlov's dog when women give me even the slightest encouragement.

Twenty seconds later and I'm on my way to my truck, all while kicking myself.

THREE

KELLY

With Zac sent away with a flea in his ear, I head back to the kitchen. I need to deal with the leftovers, if I'm to avoid facing a mess in the morning.

There's nothing organized about my clean up though, with me slamming the tops back on the containers and piling them haphazardly in the fridge. I've got too much work to do to worry about how Instagram-worthy it all looks.

From the little I've already done to fix my woefully out-of-date website; I'll be pulling an all-nighter to get it in good enough shape for visitors in the morning.

At least this is what I hope will happen, because I'd chickened out somewhat on the watermark on the pet food ad. In the end, I'd made my name subtle enough it'll be missed by all but the most eagle-eyed observer.

With luck on my side, that won't include Jason Ralph, my talentless ECD, and the one who'll take the credit for my work. All I can hope is that the client is more observant than my boss.

As I take another look at the design, I can't help but feel proud. While it might be a simple ad, I like to think it'll also work its socks off. All too often, Jason would push for an 'award-winning' design. It'd also be one that was useless in doing what the customer had asked for.

And if it won an award, it'd be one that had Jason pushing you to one side to be up on stage to collect. And he'd hold it high while he was about it.

A last critical look at the design and I close the file. "Burt, it's up to you." Of course, there might not be a 'Burt' behind Burt's Pet Food. The client could have named the product range after their kid, or even their dog, as was often the case.

As I painstakingly update my website, part of my brain is stuck on the meal I'd shared with Zac.

"Why did he have to ruin it with that stupid wink?"

My working with alpha males had turned me off flirting of that sort. Perhaps any flirting. When I'd first started in advertising, I'd found the bravado so sexy.

These days it irritates me. Are they flirting because they like me? Or do they want me moving their job to the top of the pile? Experience had shown that ninety-nine percent of the time, it was the latter.

As Zac and I had talked about the renovations over dinner, his creative ideas had me thinking he might have hidden depths. Hah, as if. That wink proved he was one of those handsome—okay, drop-dead gorgeous—guys, who expected every woman to fall at his feet.

So—not—happening. Not with a guy as cocky as Zac Thomas.

Despite going to bed around four o'clock, I didn't sleep well. My mind crowded with what I see as the slow and steady decline of my career. A call to Deb after I'd sent Zac on his way, and I knew we wouldn't be applying for jobs as a team. Not with her giving up agency life altogether.

I wish it was something I could do, but without a husband to support me, I need to keep earning and advertising is all I've ever known. I'm also stubborn as a mule and, having committed to the industry, I'm not giving up on a whim, and not because of Jason.

Fed up with tossing and turning, it was a relief to clamber out of bed when the alarm on my phone sounded. Yet, despite a blistering hot shower, and even hotter coffee, I'm no better when Zac and the others turn up for work.

That he looks well-rested and as handsome as ever has me feeling even less kindly toward him. While he's not the one responsible for the challenges I'm facing, he's on hand, making him an easier target than Jason Ralph.

If Zac so much as has a twitchy eye in my orbit, I'll ring Ethan and tell him I want Zac to be taken off the job. A final glare in his direction and I head back to my office to see if there have been any visits to my website.

Not a single one.

There isn't even an email from Jason acknowledging that he'd received my design, although I know he did because I'd requested a read receipt. I wasn't getting caught that way again.

It was for this reason I'd also copied in the account executive assigned to Burt's Pet Food. Fool me once...

More concerning than no response from either of them is that there aren't even any creative briefs in my in-box. Is that Jason's next plan? Telling me there's not enough work, so they're taking on a junior? That I'm not wanted? That I'm obsolete?

Three days with nothing from Jason and no hits on my website, and I'm getting antsy. No, that's an understatement. I'm freaking out, big time. Rather than give him a chance to say I'm not chasing work, I email him at eight every morning and again mid-afternoon.

Rather than leave it up to chance, I also copy the head of client service, making it harder for Jason to say I haven't been in touch. I've been in advertising too long and seen others targeted with constructive termination too often, not to know how to play the game. The first rule being, put everything in writing and screen-grab the jeepers out of stuff.

However, now that it's my career on the line, and not someone else's, I don't find it as fascinating as it had been when I was an observer. Rather, my heart is in my mouth as I consider my options.

While I'd been annoyed when Zac first removed all the kitchen cabinets, it hasn't bothered me since. With my stomach in knots, I've been living on soup and toast when I can gag it down.

Two more days pass during which I continue adding yet more examples to my website. I've even surprised myself with the quality and quantity of work I've produced during my time with MC&S.

Seeing it laid out like this has highlighted something I wouldn't have noticed otherwise. Since Jason started a little over eighteen months ago, the projects I've got to work on are no longer for the agency's biggest clients.

Why hadn't I seen what was happening? Too busy wrapped up in my little bubble, happy to get on with my work, and avoid the all-consuming agency politics?

Only now do I realize that while I've been working from home, the politics had continued apace. The only difference is I've been unaware of them and thus able to avoid any fallout. And now, it's too late.

Hard to believe now that the women at the agency had been abuzz on hearing there was fresh blood arriving from the Sydney office.

Sadly, on an Aussie ranking of box jellyfish to Chris Hemsworth, Jason, being venomous and lacking any muscle tone, was at the invertebrate end of the scale.

Perhaps even more upsetting than letting a low-life like him ruin my career is the drop off in my own projects courtesy of this creative suffocation. I haven't picked up a paintbrush in months, let alone thought about starting a new painting.

ZAC

Despite telling myself that Kelly-Stuck-Up Sanderson is a lost cause, she still draws my gaze. Not that I see much of her over the following days with her sticking to her office at the front of the house.

She isn't even using the kitchen much, with the microwave having disappeared from atop the pile of cabinets. I guess I can't blame her for moving it. We're kicking up a heap of dust as we dismantle the back of the house.

With the deck rebuilt, we've moved onto framing out the opening for the doors into the large family room that looks over the backyard. We're close to fitting the sliders when Josh Kendrick, who's on site giving us a hand, glances in the kitchen window.

"What the hell, Zac? I thought Tyler said you weren't due to start demo in there until we sorted out the deck and all the new doors?"

I don't bother going into detail. "One of them fell off the wall, so I took the rest down. They were a freaking accident waiting to happen." There's no need to allude to earthquakes, with Mother Earth choosing that very moment to shimmy.

The site falls silent, but for the battered and paint-splattered radio that's tuned to the local station. As always, we wait to see if this is the big one that we keep hearing about. When we realize it's not, the banter and work kick off again.

Josh tips his head toward the kitchen. "I'll get Tyler to put a rush on those new cabinets. You know how Ethan is about leaving clients stuck like this. I'll go see if she's happy for us to move on that now, rather than wait until we've closed in the back."

There isn't a chance I want Josh Kendrick going anywhere near Kelly. While he might be a moody bastard on occasions, there's something guarded about him that has women all over him like a rash.

Instead of giving him a chance to move, I shove my drill at him, with him having no option but to grab hold of it. "I'll go."

Not giving him time to argue, I take off, with his grumbling dogging my steps. Despite wanting to see Kelly, I've also wanted a good excuse because nothing has a guy looking more pathetic than a fake reason for visiting.

Image is everything when you're chatting up women.

I've no sooner had this thought than shame spikes in my chest. However, I don't allow myself to examine it, rather knocking on the front door more forcefully than intended. As well as being quicker and easier than using the backdoor, it'll mean Josh, and the others can't hang on my every word.

I sense something is wrong as soon as Kelly opens the door. This makes no sense. As a Californian native, she should be used to earthquakes, especially mini shakes, like the one we've just had. And yet, she appears badly rattled.

"Are you alright?"

She looks ready to speak, but eventually shakes her head, the action uncoordinated.

With the challenge that's often present in her eyes, missing in action, I don't think twice, stepping forward and pulling her in for a hug. While it starts out as it had on the day that she'd come close to being taken out by that cabinet, this doesn't last.

I'd have to be dead to ignore Kelly's body tight up against mine, her unique perfume filling my senses. We fit together perfectly, as if forming two halves of a puzzle. A complicated puzzle I've yet to fathom.

However, there's nothing complicated about the way my body reacts to her nearness. My breathing stutters, my cock twitches, and I'm filled with a desire to go full cave man and protect this striking woman at all costs.

Even from yourself?

I pull back, taking us both by surprise. As experienced as I am, there's no missing her arousal, her eyes dark with passion and the promise of more. Meanwhile, her lips are parted and just begging for me to claim them.

It would be so easy to wrap my arms back around her, and to ...

The thought of driving myself into her lush depths while she screamed my name has me taking an even bigger step backwards. If only it was as easy to rid myself of the desire to take her every which way but sideways.

Okay, sideways can be fun, too.

"Kelly, it wasn't a big earthquake. Everything is okay out the back." At her confusion, I press on. "Anyway, I just wanted to know if it's alright if we move ahead with the kitchen rebuild?"

She nods, with this as uncoordinated as her head shake had been earlier. I'm about to return to work, when I change my mind.

"Are you sure there's nothing I can help with?"

It would appear not, although this doesn't stop her from blurting out the issues she's facing at work. Her boss sounds like an asshole. And while she's right that I can't help there, this doesn't mean I don't have advice.

"Have you thought about picking up some side jobs? At least until things return to normal."

Kelly's expression says she's not convinced.

"That's all good in theory. But advertising is close-knit. If word got out that I was freelancing while still employed, I'd be fired so fast my head would spin."

Now I'm the one who's confused. "But aren't you in danger of losing your job, anyway?" I pause before adding, "Anything has to be better than those bastards giving you the runaround. Do you want to give them the satisfaction?"

It's not until I'm at the bottom of the front steps and she's about to close the door that I comment.

"If it was me, I'd prefer to go out in a blaze of glory."

The response I get to this idea is her shutting the door and putting an end to our conversation. Damn it, the woman needs help to see she could use her talent in so many ways.

That dog roll advertisement had been funny as hell. And clever, beyond all else, it was clever. Something that would have it standing out amongst the trash that often popped up in whatever I was trying to scroll online.

It's on remembering the homemade flyer I'd found under the wiper of my truck a couple of days back that a plan forms. It'll be one that has Kelly focusing on something more positive than the end of her career in advertising.

And, if I play it right, it'll be one that uses her creative skills, and that has me tight by her side when it happens. First thing I'll be doing when I get home is raiding the recycling to find that flyer. There had to be a phone number or contact information for the organizers on there somewhere.

FOUR

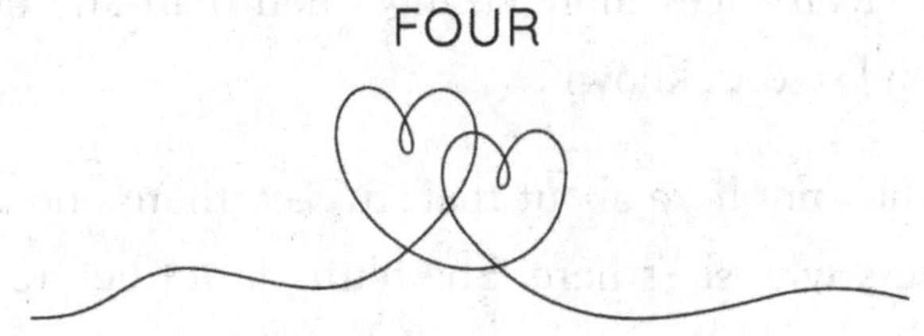

KELLY

The following morning and I've been sitting waiting for over-an-hour for signs of life from the agency.

I'm still waiting when there's a knock at the front door. I doubt it's any of the Lucky Break crew, with them all banging and crashing either out back, or in the kitchen.

Rather than it being Zac checking to see if they're being too loud, it's Mary Miller, our neighbor, and Chairman of the Neighborhood Watch. I'm not sure why she's here, because I'd let her know about the renovations.

Better to give her a heads up than have her phoning my mom every time there's a 'strange man' lurking about. Mary sees more strange men than any other person I've ever known.

But she's not here about that. In fact, there's no time to guess why she's here. She blurts it out before I've so much as said good morning.

"I need your help, dear girl."

If I actually had some agency work to get on with, I'd be back-pedaling by now, telling her I was too busy. However, that excuse has bolted. "Really?"

It's not until I notice her fidgeting that I think to invite her inside.

Only once we're settled with coffee in what my parents refer to as the front parlor, does she get around to why she's here.

"It's the 4th of July. Normally my Barry would take care of our Neighborhood Watch float for the Independence Day Parade, but with his health playing up, I don't want to risk it."
She then sits quietly, waiting for me to pick up the sympathy card she's just dealt me. Perhaps if Barry

spent more time actually playing tennis than watching it on TV while cradling a beer, his health would be better.

Of course, I say nothing of this. The poor woman has enough to deal with babysitting her husband of forty-odd years. Eventually, though, curiosity gets the better of me.

"How do you expect me to help? I wouldn't know the first thing about building a float."

I'd back this up by offering the excuse that I'm in full-time employment, but as each hour passes with no emails, even this is in doubt. Maybe I should look for freelance work like Zac said?

"No, no, no, dear girl, you just need to come up with a design. Others can build it using the same trailer as last year."

While my immediate reaction is to tell her no. I then decide the idea of working on something Jason can't take the credit for would make a welcome change. It'll also be the first time I've been in town for the famous parade, so I may as well make the most of it.

If it turns out great, I can even put it on my website.

And because it's a charity job, there's nothing Jason can say about it.

"Are there any rules I should follow?"

I'm used to working to a brief, no matter how 'brief' it might occasionally be. I've found it's best to have some guidelines, things I can and can't do, otherwise I have a tendency to get carried away.

Mary thinks on this, shaking her head as she goes through some internal list. "Kelly, whatever you come up with will be wonderful. Just make it family friendly, is all." She quiets for a moment. "Oh, you'll need to make sure it's got the Neighborhood Watch branding on it."

"That actually sounds like a lot of fun." I fall silent while searching for negatives, soon enough deciding there aren't any. "Okay, I'll do it. I'm in."

"Would it also be possible for you to manage the project so I can devote more time to taking care of Barry?"

I'm soon enough nodding, although I then back this up by saying I'll manage it for her. I mean, it can't be any harder than some of the crap jobs Jason had foisted on me in recent months, can it?

"That's excellent news. Can you whip something up within a couple of days?"

With my mind already awhirl with design options, it takes a moment to realize she's spoken to me. "Sorry, what was that?"

"A couple of days. Would that be enough time?"

"That should be plenty. I'll get started right away."

It wasn't like I had anything else to do.

She's out the front door, and obviously eager to be on her way, when she stops briefly.

"I'd better get home. Time for Barry's back rub. When you're ready, we can talk it through with the nice young man who's put his hand up to help."

It's a tossup what grabs my attention first. Her massaging her husband, her suddenly florid complexion, or the real kicker. "Nice young man?"

She nods enthusiastically before gushing out, "Zac Thomas. I believe you know him?"

Sheesh, I know him alright. And it looks as if that smile and wink nonsense of his works, if the color in Mary's cheeks is anything to go by. However, I can't give her grief about that considering how I'd reacted to being plastered all over his chest yesterday.

It had taken me longer than it should to fall asleep last night thanks to him popping up every time I closed my eyes. I'd be kidding myself to ignore my attraction to him. And I'd be stupid to act on it, with heartache all I'd gain from it.

It's about now I realize, having committed to the project, that I'll be stuck working with that cocky so-and-so, at least until the 4th of July.

Of course, if I come up with a design that's bigger than Texas, he'll be too busy building to have time to hit on me. As I sit back at my desk, there's nothing I can do to stop my grin.

It's time Zac Thomas found out that after five years in advertising, I'm immune to his kind. You don't make that sort of mistake three times. I've learned my lesson. At least I hope I have.

ZAC

From the back of the property, I see Mary Miller making her way down the front steps.

Honestly, the woman is insubstantial as thistledown, and as likely to blow over in a slight breeze. Worried she'll trip over some of the debris we've left in the driveway, I waste no time racing after her.

It's always chaotic when we're waiting for a fresh dumpster. Luckily, I'm at the old lady's side before she's gone too far, my hand under her elbow gently steering her away from a haphazard pile of battered siding.

"So, how did you get on?"

She stops, turns, and beams up at me. "Kelly's such a lovely girl. She said she'll help with the design and the project, too. That's a weight off my mind."

To avoid yet another blow-by-blow account of her husband's recent passing of a kidney stone, I press on. "Did she say when she'd have a design?"

I glance up at the large front window, and despite the blind being down to stop the morning light, I know Kelly is watching me. I can sense it as surely as if she was running her hands all over my body.

Something I hope to experience firsthand in the not-to-distant future. It's a thought that has me fighting the urge to puff my chest out and smile up at her.

However, after her reaction to my innocent—okay, not so innocent—wink, I don't want to push it too hard. Thankfully, Mary starts up again, once more holding my attention.

"Kelly told me she'll have something ready in a day or two. That should give you enough time to build it, shouldn't it?"

A quick calculation of how far off the 4th of July is, and how many hours I can devote to the project at evenings and weekends, and I nod. However, it's tentative. "It should be okay, but I'll tell you once I've seen the design."

Her smile slips, and I hurry to assure her I've got plenty of people to recruit if needs be. And as if the universe was keeping an eye out for me, Tyler arrives back on site.

He's out of his truck in an instant and soon enough, stopping next to me. This leaves me with no option other than to carry out introductions.

"Tyler, I'd like you to meet Mary Miller. Mary, this is Tyler Pierce, our supervisor." I then look back at Tyler. "Mary is Kelly's neighbor, and she's got a project she needs my help with. You'd be okay with that, wouldn't you?"

He can't say no, not in front of a potential client. And because he doesn't realize it's a charity job, he even volunteers the help of others in the team. I'll deal with the fallout later, but not unless I have to.

From what I've seen, most floats are box shaped and draped in as much red, white, and blue bunting, and as many flags as we can lay our hands on. Barry, having explained over the phone that the trailer is a flat-bed, with metal railings at the front and sides, means it should be a push-over.

However, I won't know for sure until I've seen Kelly's design.

After briefly tipping his head in Mary's direction, Tyler slams his hand down on my shoulder. It's an unspoken command to stop chatting and get back to work. "Dumpster is on its way. Should be here soon."

His message delivered loud and clear, Tyler marches off up the drive and around the side of the house. "Leave it with me, Mrs. Miller. I'll check in with Kelly in a couple of days and update you after that."

The old dear rests her hand on my arm before gushing out. "That's so wonderful. It's lovely having a nice young man like you to take care of things. I remember when Barry..."

There isn't a chance I want her starting in on her memories. I'm not being sucked in that way, twice. Instead, I pat her hand, with her blushing in response as she had last time.

"You can tell me all about it when we next catch up. Meanwhile, I'd better get going before I get fired."

To an accompaniment of her giggling, I go in search of Tyler, slowing a little as I pass the front door. I'm fully expecting Kelly to corner me, with her having seen through every other ruse of mine to get closer.

Part of me would be disappointed if she didn't see through me. As I go to re-join the rest of the crew, I can't stop myself from whistling.

I've used the porta potty at the front of the property four times before I realize Kelly is ignoring me on purpose.

This has my smile widening. Love and hate are so intertwined, and it's something I'll use to my advantage.

. . .

Instead of two days, Kelly comes up with a design in one. I guess she's used to working to tight deadlines, although when I see what she's come up with, I'm pleased to have the extra day up my sleeve.

The damned design has more bells and whistles than is common on Independence Day floats. So much for my bunting and flags theory.

"It's big, I'll give it that." I tap her computer screen and am rewarded with a sharp intake of breath from Kelly. "Sorry." I yank my hand back, simply pointing this time. "These lines. Does that mean the rocket moves somehow?"

I'd sneak in some innuendo about movement, but the magnitude of what I face building, and in under four weeks at that, has robbed me of the ability to flirt.

The other worry is the miniscule budget we're dealing with. Kelly's design says she mightn't be aware of this. "Did Mary tell you how much she's got put aside for the float?"

After I tell her, Kelly is downcast, muttering about

having to start again from scratch. Given the other disappointments in her life of late, I'm not having it.

"Like hell you will. I'll make this work, somehow." I glance away from the screen, "Make that, WE'LL make it work, because I'm gonna need all the help I can get on this one."

It isn't until I smile broadly that Kelly responds in kind. And maybe it's because I'm not trying to hit on her. Rather, it's that I'm actually eager to work alongside her on the float.

On something that allows my creative skills to shine as much as hers have with the design.

FIVE

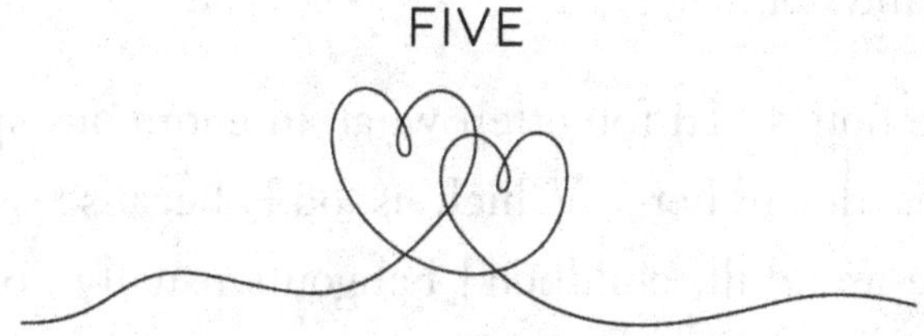

KELLY

I'm in the middle of the three-car-garage under the house when I close my eyes and breathe deeply. The memories of vacations spent here as a kid soon blind me to the modern day, with a sense of calm settling on me.

While the adults took over the house, the kids fought over who got the top bunks of the half-dozen bunk beds down here.

I wasn't one of those fighting for what was a prime position. To my mind, it had me far too close to the spiders that lurked in the exposed rafters, just waiting for me to fall asleep.

I could cope with the bottom bunk, if it had those eight-legged-monsters landing on one of the other kids, and not me.

To be honest, I'd forgotten what an enormous space it was down here. Which is odd, because when you're an adult, childhood hangouts usually appear smaller.

Of course, until now, I was coming or going, my car taking up most of the space. With my Tesla out in the driveway, there's plenty of floor space for Zac and me to spread out.

The only thing that appears unchanged is the head-height. Despite all of this, I'm still not sure what made me suggest we construct the float down here.

It was an offer Zac had jumped at, saying it would make it easier for him to get busy the moment he clocked off with Lucky Break. And while the garage is bigger than I remember—the bunk beds pushed to one side—it's still too intimate by far.

I'm not sure if I'm comfortable being in close quarters with a guy as undeniably attractive as this one. Okay, he's hotter than hell, and exactly the sort I've made the mistake of trying for in the past.

I've come to no decision when I sense movement behind me, something that has me spinning around. It's Zac, a fact I'd instinctively known thanks to the hairs on the back of my neck standing up.

On him joining me, I've got goosebumps all over my body. It doesn't matter that mom and dad insulated and carpeted the space so it could do double-duty as the kids' area. My reaction has nothing to do with temperature, unless you count my libido firing up despite my best intentions.

Zac is relaxed in comparison, holding a plastic lunchbox in one hand and a half-eaten sandwich in the other. It's lunchtime? A check of my watch tells me it's actually closer to dinnertime.

Out on the street, Zac's truck sits alone at the curb. As wrapped up as I'd been in my own worries, I hadn't noticed everyone else leaving.

Rather, I've spent the afternoon changing things on my website that didn't need changing. Anything to avoid focusing on the end of my career. The death spirals of worry getting worse by the minute. I'd decided it was better to prepare for the float.

Anything beat sitting at my computer, powerless.

Even away from my desk, I'm consumed with worry. It therefore takes me longer than it should to see that Zac's truck isn't parked where it had been earlier.

He'd left and come back? Why would he do that? He'd told me he wasn't in a relationship, and my gut told me he was telling the truth. So why leave if you plan on returning?

He swings his sandwich around, taking in the full space. "This will be perfect for the components." After checking out the spider Nirvana just overhead, he frowns. "But we'll need to find somewhere else to put everything together."

And he's got the right of it, thanks to the overall height of the flamboyant design I'd come up with. As familiar as I am with it, I don't even need to close my eyes to see it clearly in my mind's eye. Focused as I am, I don't realize he's offering me the other half of his sandwich until he waves it right under my nose.

"Thanks, I'm good." My response is as automatic as it ever was at any catered meetings at the agency. It was a habit I'd gotten into back then, sick of the pitying glances if I so much as nibbled on a rice thin.

"Come on, eat it. Get some meat on those bones."

I take a second to decipher what he's meant. And even then, I don't believe it. Part of me *can't* believe it.

There's no way he'd be interested in a curvy woman. Apparently, I haven't kept my skepticism to myself with him bursting out laughing, nearly dropping the remains of his sandwich. I'm bristling before I realize he's not laughing at me.

"Hey, what can I say? I like a woman with curves." His eyelid flickers briefly, although he stops a full-blown wink. He then shrugs before adding. "I like something to hang onto."

I've not worked out how I'm supposed to respond to a comment like that, when there's a warbled "Yoo-hoo," from out front. Zac and I turn in tandem to see Mary Miller weaving her way up the cobbled driveway.

She's still aways away when Zac tips his head closer to mine, so he can keep his voice down. "Whatever you do, don't ask about Barry's kidney stones."

Then it's all I can do to keep a straight face AND breathe. The one thing I'm unsure of is whether this is down to his cheeky remark, or having that much testosterone up close and personal.

Mary's arrival left me unsure of how I felt.

"I'm so pleased I've caught you both. Here's the key."

She holds this out to Zac, who takes it automatically, even if he looks to be as unsure as I am what the key is actually for.

"It's for the storage unit where Barry parks the trailer that we use for all the floats. He'd get it himself, but his health isn't..."

Zac and I talk over each other and Mary in our desperation to avoid anything to do with Barry's bodily functions, or lack thereof.

After stammering, "I'll just show you the designs," I take my phone out of the pocket of my jeans. I'm soon flicking through the mountain of images on my phone, desperate to find the sketches I'd sent to my mom for a second opinion.

This also has me remembering what mom said about the parade. Word is that while the kids from the neighborhood used to ride on the float, these days they won't go near it. Something about Barry being a bit of a Drill Sargent.

This doesn't surprise me, with him often yelling at us kids to get off his lawn.

While I continue searching for the sketches I'd made, Zac puts his hand on Mary's arm and hits her with a look straight out of Puss in Boots. It's one that has the older lady blushing and stuttering, with all thoughts of Barry's kidney stones, forgotten.

"Where exactly is the storage unit, Mary? I can collect the trailer this evening."

She's not answered him when I'm shoving my phone under her nose, hoping to distract her further. Zac's warning was the first I'd heard of actual kidney stones, and I wanted to make it the last.

However, the woman is tenacious with her husband's health and we have to sidestep a couple more opening gambits. Eventually though, she confirms she loves the float idea to bits, and gives Zac the address of the storage unit.

Even better is when he says he'll help her walk back down the driveway because I'm having trouble holding in my laughter. The second he walks back into the garage, I hit the button to close the door.

Then we laugh until our sides hurt.

ZAC

I haven't busted a gut laughing like this in ages and while I'm enjoying it, part of me is wracked with guilt. "I shouldn't laugh, not really. But I swear that woman is like a Rottweiler when it comes to telling me about Barry's health."

Kelly looks up at me, all the while fluttering her lashes. "I don't think it's Barry's health she's most interested in."

"You're not wrong. I have to fight the urge to check my shorts for dollar bills after she corners me." Then, making the most of Kelly's good mood, I hold the keys up and jangle them. "Shall we?"

Kelly then does an even better impression of her elderly neighbor by coloring up, as though I've just suggested we get a motel together. Not a bad idea, although not one I'm pushing. At least not yet.

I rattle the keys again. "The sooner we collect the trailer, the sooner we'll know how much space we've got to play with. Unless she gave you the size of the trailer?"

Kelly shakes her head before speaking. "I asked, but she just said it was big." She looks around the garage before carrying on. "What if it doesn't fit?"

It does, but only just, leaving me to wonder about what Mary describes as Barry's 'enormous' kidney stones. They must be the size of grapefruit to impress the old girl.

After I unhitch the trailer from my truck, Kelly and I stand and take it in. It's a flat-bed monster that will be perfect to build on. It'll also mean the design will end up gigantic.

As she walks about the bare trailer, she nibbles on her bottom lip. It's not until she's back next to me she huffs out in frustration. "I'll have to scale back the design."

"What! Why?"

She flings her arms out to the sides, taking in the enormous expanse of plywood in front of us. "I know you said not to worry, but there isn't a chance we can build what I've come up with and not blow the budget."

"You're approaching this all wrong." When she turns to stare at me, I press on. "This isn't one of your fancy advertising campaigns. It has to last four hours, tops."

It's fascinating watching her thought process, with her soon enough moving on from it being an impossibility to the possibilities being endless. This has me glancing down at the phone stuffed in the back pocket of her jeans. Okay, and I check her ass out while I'm at it. I'd be stupid not to.

"Can I see your designs again?"

While she gets her phone out and finds them, I grab my tape measure to confirm the actual size of the trailer. Twenty feet long by seven feet wide, with a double axel.

By my reckoning, this will have the height of the float sitting around fifteen-feet off the ground when the rocket is at its highest. "We could even win the prize for the biggest float!"

This grabs Kelly's attention, her phone forgotten as she stares up at me, a strange light in her eyes. "There are prizes?"

As I rattle through the awards for biggest to smallest and on to unique, that strange light intensifies. After

I mention the TOP FLOAT prize, she's a woman on a mission. It's not something I've experienced before.

And damn if it isn't a turn-on. My usual dates are pliable rather than a challenge, with Kelly looking like she'll be the latter. She's now back to scrolling through the images on her phone, all while muttering to herself.

In the end, she holds it out, showing me the one Mary likes best. Taking my cue from her 'win at all costs' attitude, I rattle through how we can cobble everything together.

If I thought she was fired up before, it's nothing to her attitude now.

"Okay, I'm on it. Between Craigslist, the local charity shops and that wrecker's yard at the edge of town, I should be able to get hold of everything." After this, she kicks me out, because she's, "got work to do!"

Her giving me the heave ho wasn't what I'd planned on. And given her grandiose design, I'll be lucky to sleep during the construction phase, let alone have time to flirt. Just what a fire cracker she is, is confirmed when the next day there is a flurry of deliveries.

. . .

On entering the garage on my return to the site after work that day, I'm stunned. From empty but for the trailer, it's now full up to the rafters. It's organized though, I'll give Kelly that.

"How did you get on with getting hold of everything?" While waiting for her to respond, I take a sizeable chunk out of my sandwich, hungry as always. With Kelly nearby, the sandwich isn't all I'm hungry for.

A brief gesture to the odds and ends stacked in neat piles around the garage, and she goes through everything. "I did, as well as all this leftover ducting from Ethan. He also gave me some silver insulation paper for the exterior and LED lights for all the control panels."

After tipping a half-roll of insulation paper to one side, she reveals a teetering pile of small battery-powered fans. "I even got these off Craigslist."

Despite being unsure how she plans on using them, her enthusiasm says I'll soon find out, and I chuckle before swallowing my bite. "You've gone all out, huh?"

She shrugs, a mischievous grin spreading across her face. "To win the top prize, our rocket needs to be as spectacular as possible, right?"

Curiosity sparked, I set down my lunchbox. "What do you have in mind?"

This has her crouching next to a large plastic container of fabrics, the most common colors being red, white and blue as I've expected. However, after sorting through them, she's soon holding up a vibrant orange piece.

"We can have fake flames coming out of the rocket. The small fans will create movement."

There's no hiding my disappointment, although I try. "That's a great idea, but couldn't we have actual flame? I can hook up a couple of blowtorches. It'd be epic."

Her mouth falls open at my suggestion. "You're kidding, right?" She drops the piece of orange material atop the more patriotic fabrics. "If we do that, we'll risk setting fire to the float."

"Damn it, you're right." I don't bother trying to hide my grin. "It'd be impressive, though."

Her expression softens when she pats my shoulder, with this the first time she's touched me without being upset. "Trust me, Zac, between us, the rocket will be out of this world."

It's when I see a flicker of determination in her eyes I realize it'll be alright. Despite her knocking back my idea of actual flame, there's no denying her passion and drive.

It's a combination I hope to exploit over the next three-and-a-half weeks, and if I have my way, there'll be flame aplenty.

SIX

KELLY

As the sun dips below the horizon, and the sky is painted orange and pink, I'm once again in the three-car garage beneath Sand 'O' Sun. Whereas in the past I'd have been hanging out with my cousins playing endless games of cards, I'm now working side-by-side with Zac.

We're inching forward with our *Out of this World* float for the upcoming parade, and I couldn't be happier. Without this to fill my days, I'd have been in a bad place, eaten up by worry at the complete absence of creative briefs from Jason.

Even the account executive I work most often with is ghosting me, although I don't know why. We've always worked well together with my concepts, often proceeding straight to final art with no need for him to do a hard-sell with the client.

It was the threat of losing my job that had me saying yes when my neighbor in LA asked if her cousin could sublet my apartment. Just for a couple of months, until she found something else. I was all for it. Apart from it being safer to have someone staying there, the rent will come in handy.

As the days passed, Zac's abilities around the construction of the float continued to amaze me. This was a surprise after seeing him swing a hammer with wild abandon out back.

However, working this closely with him, there's no missing his creativity and ingenuity. This is especially so when you consider the jetsam and flotsam that we're stuck with, thanks to Mary's miniscule budget.

Zac's nimble fingers dance across the tools, shaping and molding the float's framework with precision.

Every stroke and twist effortless, as if he possesses an innate connection with his craft. I watch in awe as he brings my complex ideas to life, transforming them into something extraordinary.

"Wow, that's amazing." Unable to contain my admiration any longer, I add, "I didn't know you were so talented," while doing my best to keep from going full fangirl. However, his crooked smile, and eyes sparkling with a mixture of pride and mischief, tell me I've failed miserably.

"Thanks. I have a talent for working with my hands. I love figuring out how to make everything fit together."

Despite a heaping dollop of innuendo, his words still resonate with me. I also can't help but draw parallels between his craftsmanship and the way he carries himself.

He exudes a quiet confidence that has eluded me until now, with me too busy looking out for hints I'm being played. It's as if I've discovered a whole extra layer to Zac, and it's one I'm finding hard to resist.

His flirting is something he does without thinking, coming as naturally as breathing. I'd be kidding myself if I thought there was anything in it. And even then, I wouldn't act on it. Not with a charmer, like him.

However, as the days pass and our evenings are consumed by the float, Zac and I grow closer. We share laughter, conversations, and moments of vulnerability.

It's during one of these candid exchanges he leans in closer, his voice dropping to a low, suggestive whisper.

"You know, Kelly, my skills aren't confined to the garage." There's no missing the dirty glint in his eyes, with a resultant rush of heat coursing through my veins.

Blast him. I thought we'd put this behind us, allowing me to relax rather than stress about him being here for a good time, rather than a long time. I hoped he'd see me as more than a conquest as we got to know each other.

Looks like he's reverted to form, with his words carrying a hint of seduction and the promise of passion beneath their playful nature. My heart stutters, and I can't deny the growing desire that simmers within me.

Does that mean I'm acting on it? Heck no, it doesn't. I've got enough troubles in my life without succumbing to his advances.

"That's a bold claim, Zac."

There's a hard edge to my voice, because I don't need this in my topsy-turvy world.

He chuckles, closing the gap between us. "Oh, I assure you, it's one I can prove. I love a challenge, and baby, you're all that, and more."

I feign nonchalance, crossing my arms and trying to suppress the rising anticipation. "Is that so? Well, good luck with that. I'm not easily swayed."

Zac's gaze intensifies, locking with mine in a silent battle of wills. "We'll see about that, Kelly. We'll see."

As the days turn into weeks, his interactions grow bolder, filled with lingering glances and subtle touches. Each passing moment makes it harder to keep him at arm's length, the magnetic pull growing stronger. The lines blur, and the boundaries I've set to protect myself are showing signs of wear.

The float becomes more than a project; it becomes a symbol of the connection we're building. Busy in the dimly lit garage, the smell of paint in the air, I wonder if the sparks ignited here will find their way into other aspects of our lives.

I find out after finishing the fabric 'flames' and turning on the little fans. While not as authentic as Zac's blowtorches would have been, they pass muster.

Without warning, Zac picks me up and swings me around in celebration. And it could have ended there, if not for my gaze landing on his lips when he slides me down his body and back to my feet.

In a moment of lunacy, I surrender. I'm sick of fighting my attraction to him. Instead, my reticence is overcome with lust. Rampant lust of the sort to have those fake flames going up in smoke. The sort that has me reaching up on tiptoes and mashing my lips against his.

What starts out as a celebratory kiss is soon less about

celebration and more in line with copulation. And it's all on me.

What I'm thinking when I run my tongue across his lips, I don't know. I can try fooling myself that it was automatic, but even I'm not that gullible.

As his tongue tangles with mine, I melt against him, rational thoughts as lost as I am to the moment. Instead, my world centers on where our lips and bodies touch.

I'm fully into it when what had been a niggling thought takes form. There's no way a guy kisses like this without a heap of practice.

I'm doubtless one of dozens of women who've tasted this man's sweet lips, flooding me with performance anxieties. I'm nowhere near as practiced as he obviously is. What if I'm doing it wrong? What if he thinks I'm a slobbering mess?

I break our kiss and stagger back, all the while wiping my lips. Not in disgust, but hoping to dull the tingling that shows every sign of taking over my body.

My kiss, lacking finesse as it must have, would be bad enough, without adding to my embarrassment by showing him how it's affected me.

"Let's forget that just happened. It's been a long week. I'm um, yeah, I'll just..."

Despite my not managing a complete sentence, Zac gets the message. His gaze sharpens, his lips tighten, and the humor that lights him up from inside is snuffed out.

Without saying goodbye, he hightails it out to his truck and is soon roaring off down the road. The garage falls silent but for the hum of the fans.

That is until I hear an all too familiar, "Yoo-hoo." Despite my desire to close the garage door and hide from the world, I can't. It's not Mary's fault I feel awful. And anyway, a blow-by-blow account of Barry's kidney stones will take my mind off what a fool I've just made of myself.

Whether it will rid me of the ugly little voice telling me I've led Zac on, that I'm not so sure about. And anyway, him not being interested in anything long term, he'll get over it, perhaps quicker than I will?

ZAC

On pulling into the driveway at my place, I'm no

clearer about what just happened with Kelly. She'd been into it. There was no doubting that.

Hell, she started our kiss, and there was nothing casual about the way she ran her tongue across the crease of my lips. If it was the other way around, I could understand her changing her mind.

However, I've never forced myself on a woman and don't intend to. Most of the time, the problem was fending them off.

So why then do I desire the one woman who doesn't want me in return? Beyond my help on the float, that is. There's a moment's remorse when I remember the reason that she's stuck working on it is because of my interference.

Will I even be welcome back on site, let alone allowed in the garage?

I guess I'll find out in the morning. It being Saturday, my only reason to be there will be to work on the float, with Kelly quite within her rights, to tell me to get lost.

I'm staring at the microwave while I nuke something to eat, when I decide I can't wait. I can't leave things as they are. Kelly doesn't deserve me storming off into the night.

I'm also intrigued by what a proper relationship with Kelly would be like. My last long-term relationship was ...

The microwave dings and I give up trying to work out when it was. It was a long time ago. Perhaps too long.

And, if I'm honest with myself, sleep won't come easy if I'm thinking about what went wrong. Soon enough, I'm back at Kelly's after gobbling a lasagna that had been hotter than the sun.

Seeing the garage door shut comes as no surprise. However, there are no lights showing, other than the one on the front porch. That's not right. I've never seen the home as dark as it is now.

Not content with driving away, I park my truck, worry gnawing at the pasta meal now sitting in my gut like a brick. I'd rather risk Kelly yelling at me to get lost than not take the time to check she's all right.

She's not out for the evening, because her car sits in the driveway. There's nothing tentative about my knock on her front door, with it loud enough to wake the dead.

I've been hammering for five minutes before I accept the door won't be opened. Short of breaking in, or calling the cops, there's nothing else I can do. I don't even have her phone number, with her saying it wasn't necessary. And I sure can't ask Ethan for it.

The less he knows about how much time I'm spending with Kelly after hours, the more likely I am to keep my job. While easy-going, he didn't want us fooling around with clients.

I'd argue that all I'm doing is helping Kelly with the float, but I'm not that convincing a liar. If he pressed me on it, I'd have to tell him the truth, and that's something I'm not ready to face myself.

Worrying about a woman is an alien emotion, and not because I don't care for the women I date. It's more that I never date them long enough to form a genuine bond.

The realization that I've done so with Kelly hits me like a ton of bricks, similar to that in my gut. I might even care for her enough to risk my job.

I'm back at my truck, ready to ring Tyler for Kelly's number, when I look up at the house next door. Unlike Kelly's place, every light on offer appears to be working over at Mary's.

And, the old girl being the busy body that she is, if anyone knows where Kelly is and whether she's okay, it'll be Mary. It's enough to have me shoving my keys in the back pocket of my jeans and making straight for the brightly lit front porch.

While I try to temper my enthusiasm, my knock is still loud, with the old lady answering the door soon after, worry marring her sweet face. Thankfully, this disappears when she sees that it's me.

"Why, if it isn't young, Zac Thomas? Kelly was just telling me how you're progressing with the float. Come in. Come in. You'll join us for dinner, won't you? There's plenty to go around."

Despite my having just eaten, I accept, because it will give me a chance to test the waters with Kelly and see for myself, that she's okay. Of course, it'll also mean I can't ask her what happened earlier with that kiss.

When I think about it, that might not be a bad thing. Especially when I see Kelly sitting at a dinner table crowded with good china, candles, and a truck-load of cutlery. While it's formal, I get it isn't unusual in this household.

An elderly gent, I assume is Barry, sits at the head of the table, at ease with the over-the-top set-up. He also appears in rude good health for someone battling kidney stones.

However, Kelly looks on edge, although this might be because I've rocked up uninvited, rather than her worrying about which knife and fork to use.

After setting a place for me across from Kelly, Mary disappears into the kitchen to get a plate of food for me. Although not before telling me to, "Sit down and make yourself comfy."

Now there's no avoiding the sadness in Kelly's eyes. And blast, if I'm not responsible somehow. I'm therefore confused when I see the worry replaced with something approaching glee when Mary puts a heaping plate of food down in front of me.

"I hope you like meatballs because Barry doesn't have much of an appetite tonight. And I wasn't aware

Kelly was a vegetarian until I was serving up. Still, that's extra meatballs for a growing boy like you."

This leaves me metaphorically scratching my head. While I can understand Barry being off his food if he's unwell, there's no way Kelly is a vegetarian. We've shared enough meat lover's pizza and green chicken curries while working on the float to understand that.

Why had she told Mary she was?

I find out when I come close to cracking a tooth on the first meatball. At least I think it's a meatball, because the blasted thing has more in common with kidney stones than fine cuisine.

At least now I know why Kelly is choking down laughter along with mashed potatoes that have a lot in common with spackle.

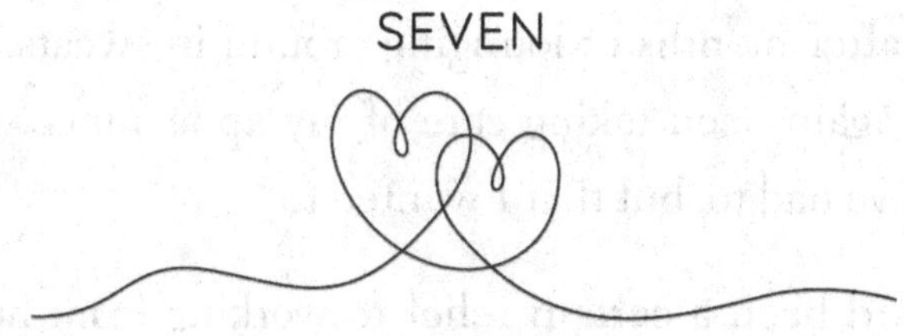

SEVEN

KELLY

I'd only said yes to Mary's invitation to dinner because I couldn't stand being alone after Zac took off. Better I allow my neighbor to take charge, so I can avoid focusing on what an ass I'd made of myself over him.

Girls like me don't make the first move and kiss guys like him. Not without risking heartache or ridicule. So much for all those pep talks I'd given myself over the years to not fall for the hot guy.

Yet here I am, again, with my heart rate hitting triple digits whenever Zac is nearby. My libido is sitting up and taking notice after years of having its nose stuffed in a book, and my dreams are full of tender moments.

And after months of lounging around in sweats, I've once again been taking care of my appearance. Not that I've had to, but that I wanted to.

There'd been a certain relief to working from home and being able to dress as I liked. So much easier than trying my best to find haute couture for curvy girls with this almost an oxymoron.

I'd found a few designers, but it wasn't easy keeping up with the other women at the agency.

Why then did I try to fashion myself as if I was like them? That I could attract a guy as hot as Zac.

Hopeless, hopeless, hopeless.

All of this is going through my head as I watch Zac valiantly trying to eat those meatballs. On seeing the size of them when Mary was bustling around in the kitchen, I knew they'd be as hard as bullets.

Better to embrace vegetarianism than hurt her feelings. However, as I struggle through the mashed 'wood filler' and Brussels sprouts that should have stayed in that fine city, I regret not telling her I was on a fast.

What can I say? I wasn't thinking straight after Zac took off. With him back again and sitting across from me, I'm still not thinking straight. When he'd sped off, he'd shown no signs of returning before the next day, if ever.

And who could blame him, with me throwing myself at him uninvited? Even putting the food to one side, which I have to, the meal is an ordeal.

Zac's gaze only strays from mine, when he's asked a direct question, with most of these coming from Mary. Meanwhile, Zac questions me, with glances and the occasional quirking of an eyebrow, leaving me struggling to know what he wants. Or worse, what I want.

An eternity has passed before Mary clears the plates and asks if we'd like dessert.

Having seen it, I'm quick to say no, and that I'm stuffed. Zac, who's looking a little green, follows suit. We repeat the process when our lovely hostess asks if we'd like coffee and cake instead.

"Mary, I'd love to, but I'm on deadline and coffee keeps me awake." I pat her arm to soften the blow of my turning down her kind offer.

Likewise, Zac tells her he has to get up early the next morning, but that it's been a lovely meal. Soon enough, we're out front, Mary waving before disappearing back inside to continue attending to Barry's every need.

As we walk back up the sidewalk to Sand 'O' Sun, Zac is the first to speak.

"You know Barry's health? I don't think it's kidney stones at all."

Thanks to the streetlight out front of my place, I'm able to see he's quite serious about this.

"Really? What do you think it is?"

Zac's top lip curls before he answers me. "Undigested meatballs!" He then laughs, to the point he's bent double.

Soon enough, I'm laughing right along with him. "Were they as bad as they looked?"

Zac takes his time getting his laughter under control.

"I reckon Barry's kidney stones would be easier to chew!"

He then takes me by surprise, by throwing his arm around my shoulder and squeezing me close. He follows this up by kissing the top of my head, easy enough with him so much taller.

"Kelly, I'm sorry if I upset you earlier."

Wait? What? He's sorry that he upset me? But he had nothing to do with me throwing myself at him. That was all on me. While it would be easy enough to accept his apology, I can't. Not when I'm the one at fault.

"No Zac, I'm the one who should be apologizing. I should never, ah, I, ah ... I'm so very sorry."

Rather than accept the apology, he steers me up my driveway, his arm still slung across my shoulders. As we stroll side-by-side, I relax, his embrace friendly, but nothing more.

This is a relief, because despite my attraction to him being one-sided, I value his friendship. Rather than working on the float in silence, we've connected at a deeper level, talking of our hopes and dreams.

When I first met him, I'd never have picked him for a guy who wanted to have his own business restoring furniture, but there you go. Even hotties have hidden depths.

He'd shared that with me when I'd told him more of what I was facing at the agency. After taking the time to digest it, he'd agreed with me that Jason was out to get me.

On reaching the front door, I slide my key into the lock, step inside, and turn to face him before speaking. "I'll see you in the morning. Again, I'm so sorry..."

I don't finish yet another apology for my behavior, with Zac reaching up and putting his finger over my lips. "Shhh, don't. You don't need to apologize for something I've wanted myself for weeks."

I'm still processing his words when he places his hands gently on either side of my head, leans in, and brushes his lips over mine. The kiss is ethereal, as though he isn't sure of himself.

That doesn't last long past my stepping forward to be closer to him. It's something that has me missing the edge of the doorsill and slamming against him. His arms wrap tight around me, pulling me closer.

As my heart opens to him, so do my lips, his tongue playing with mine, resulting in heat pooling between my thighs. And I'm not alone in my reaction, with his erection soon enough nudging my tummy.

Despite my body being into it, I can't shut my brain up. It's rabbiting on about him being too hot for me, distracting me from the kiss. Soon enough, Zac notices my inattention and lifts his head.

The fire in his eyes is more than a match for the fire in my body, easing my worries. It's enough to convince me to put my hand behind his head and bring his lips back down to mine.

My emotions toward this gorgeous man are enough to have me throwing caution to the wind. Even if I'll regret it later, the memories of a night with him will be worth it.

At least I hope so. I need a break for once in my life. Sex as a distraction? Now there's something I never thought would cross my mind.

ZAC

As Kelly's lips soften beneath mine, I have to fight the longing to devour her. I've found her attractive right from the start, but as I've got to know her better, that attraction has intensified.

It's a novel experience, with me more often having the most basic level of communication with the women I end up with. Again, I'm not full of myself in thinking this, with them as likely to want to keep any relationship...

What's the word I'm looking for?

That's right, shallow!

Kelly having shared her hopes and dreams with me, there's nothing shallow about my attraction to her. The one thing I'm unsure of is whether she's like all those other women and only after a physical relationship.

For the first time in my adult life, this doesn't sit well. Does this mean I'll turn her down? Hell no. I'm thinking this right until she leads me over to the stairs.

Now I'm torn. If I ask if we can take things slowly, she'll think I've changed my mind, that I don't find her attractive, when this is so not true.

Up in what must be the master suite, I'm at first distracted by the lights of Coogan's Break spread out before us.

It must be a killer view during the day, although it's Kelly who draws my eye now. She looks to be having second thoughts, or it could be nerves. I want our first time together to be perfect.

With her once again tight against me, my lips again cover hers. If there's one thing that I'm good at—okay, more than good at—it's pleasuring a woman. However, the pressure is even greater when I have feelings for Kelly, beyond the physical.

I break our kiss long enough to ask, "Lights on, or off?" I never assume with women. Me, I couldn't care either way, yet tonight I long to see Kelly's face when she comes.

To have her arching under me, to watch her eyelids fluttering and her mouth forming a perfect 'O' as she fills the room with her cries of pleasure. It'd be as big a turn-on as her being wrapped tight around my length.

Rather than respond to my question, she reaches out and grabs a remote off the bedside table. A moment later, the electronic blinds on the skylight overhead slide back and the bedroom is flooded with moonlight.

While nowhere near as bright as if she'd turned on a lamp, it'll be more than enough to reveal her in all her glory spread out under me. Plenty bright enough to watch her gaze widening every time I drive myself home.

And yet, despite my having been in this very situation a hundred times before, tonight I'm conscious of wanting to make a good impression.

Although not in bed, because I've no worries about my abilities in that department. I might even be too confident, according to some women. And yet I'm nowhere near that, now. I'm as raw tonight as I was when I lost my V-card to my high school art teacher, Miss Wright.

She'd taught me a lot more than brush techniques before the principal found out and she was fired. It hadn't mattered that I'd been the one to seduce her. She still took the fall. And yet the smile she'd given me when she was escorted from the classroom said she'd had no regrets.

As I peel away Kelly's t-shirt and jeans, there's a practiced efficiency to my actions. This isn't what I want. I want tonight to be real, for us to be real, for how I perform, to not matter.

There'll be no-one holding up score cards to judge me, so why then am I so worried about it? While it would be all too easy to hide behind my carefully built persona as I have in the past, that won't work tonight.

I don't think Kelly would let me away with it.

Instead, I step away from her, mussing up my hair as I long to mess up hers. "I can't, Kelly. I can't do this."

There's no missing her shock, and yet it's this that has me realizing how she might have taken my random statement. "Sorry, it's not that I can't, but ... Can we start over?"

Kelly stands in her bra and panties, her gorgeous body calling to me while she hugs herself. Damn it,

I'm not making sense. I try again, desperate to tell her what I mean. What she means to me.

"I want it to be real with you. Not how it usually is." After this, I clamp my lips shut before I say something stupid.

After taking a calming breath in through my nose and out through pursed lips, I start up again. "Kelly, I want you to take the lead. With us, tonight."

It hasn't been easy handing over control, and when I gather the nerve to check on her, I can see I'm not alone in being out of my depth.

Her expression says that if I leave it up to her, nothing's going to happen. And if nothing happens, then tomorrow will be all kinds of awkward. Of course, this could also be the case if we go ahead.

However, it's a risk I'm prepared to take, because I'm sick of lying awake at night thinking what it would be like to bury myself in this gorgeous curvy woman. "What if we take turns?"

Her nod is jerky, but confident enough to be taken as yes, although I take her unawares when I rip my t-shirt off and flick it to the side. Much to her surprise,

I then ditch my jeans. "Hey, sweetheart, I've got some catching up to do."

It's then all I can do not to wink at her, her eyes narrow enough that I'm worried I've failed. While it takes longer than it should for us both to be naked, I wouldn't have missed it for the world.

I'm way more turned on than I'd usually be. Soon enough, the moment I've dreamed of happens. Our bodies are hard up against each other, nothing between us but the heat that has been building for weeks.

My lips pressed against her forehead, I whisper, "So beautiful," as much to myself as to her. Still not content, I follow this up with, "Beautiful inside and out."

And she is. More beautiful than any of the women I've had short-term flings with, and who I've thought were all I deserved.

And yet, Kelly doesn't believe me, her incredulity showing even in the moonlight. I'm not great with words and I don't want to argue. Rather, I lower my lips to hers once more, my hands ranging over her body, giving shape to my dreams.

EIGHT

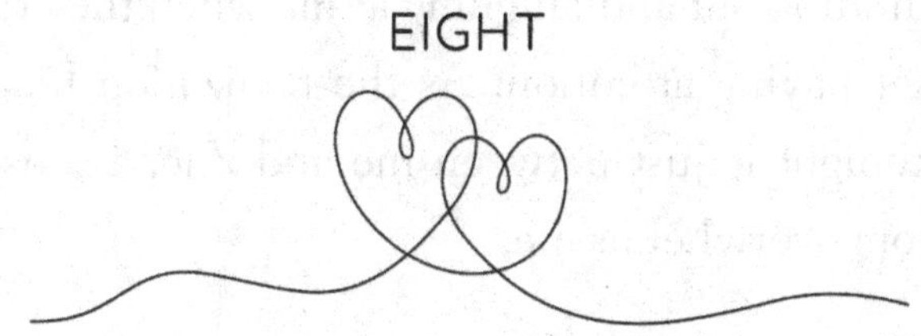

KELLY

When Zac had first suggested we take turns, I hadn't been sure, never having taken the upper hand in the bedroom. I still can't believe I kissed him earlier in the garage, feigning celebration as the reason.

What is it about Zac that has me throwing caution to the wind, and myself at him? The minute his lips touch mine, I abandon my psychoanalysis, giving myself over to our kiss.

I don't care what or even why. All I want is him consuming me, marking me as his. I don't even care if it's a case of *for now* rather than *forever*.

For once in my life, I want to experience someone screwing my brains out. No chance of anyone I work with finding out and laughing at me when they think I'm not paying attention. As the realization hits me that tonight is just between me and Zac, a sense of freedom overwhelms me.

The freedom to live for the moment rather than worry about what everyone thinks. While I have confidence in my work, the same isn't true for my body. I wish it wasn't so, but years of beating myself up for not being as thin as my co-workers have taken their toll.

With Zac's hands everywhere at once, any worries I might have soon fled, along with any inhibitions. Rather, it's as if I'm playing the part of the hot girl every guy wants, because there's no denying Zac is attracted to me.

This lends a dream-like quality to everything, our being bathed in moonlight adding to this. Before me stands a god, although one with a sinful sense of humor.

The one thing missing is his usual cockiness, with this annoying the hell out of me. Instead, he's just a regular guy, and I'm just a regular girl.

In a tumble of arms and legs on the bed, I know that's not true. There's nothing regular about Zac, especially his size. He's, um, oh my. While I don't have many lovers to compare him to, I know the moment his shaft settles on my tummy.

"I'm not sure this will work. You're so, ah, um..." I can't say it, although his wicked grin says he's got my drift.

"Hmmm, in that case, I'll just have to make you wetter, won't I?" He rubs his length back and forth through my curls. "So slick, you'll take every inch of me."

He looks ready to carry on. Instead, he bites his lip in a manner that has me wanting to do the same to him.

Only half aware of what I'm doing, I cradle his head in my hands, dragging his lips down to mine. I hunger for him as none before, and I'm over denying myself.

Soon enough, he takes control of the kiss, his tongue tangling with mine, our breath mingling, and our heartbeats matching. Mine hammers away in my chest, the pulse as strong in other parts of my body.

When Zac lifts his lips from mine, I put my hands back up to keep him where he is, although the passion in his eyes stops me. There's the promise of pleasure and more in his dark brown eyes. Pleasure that will be all mine.

And it is, with him working his way down my body, nibbling, sucking and licking until I'm a quivering wreck. I'm well on my way to being as slick as he wants when he opens me wide to his gaze.

The way his tongue twirls around my bud hints at a lot of practice, and I arch my hips, desperate to increase the pressure.

In response, his laughter rumbles against my most sensitive spot, although this soon turns to humming. Oh, my lord, at this rate, I hope he doesn't know any of the words to the song, with the vibration caused by his lips cutting right through me.

It's almost too much, my bud ready to burst into flower. Desperate to have Zac deep inside me when this happens, I grip his shoulders, trying to let him know that I'm close to losing it.

Honestly, the man appears psychic where my body is concerned. He lifts his head and slides up and along my body before kissing me, the taste of me still on his lips. Any thoughts about this vanish the moment the tip of his cock nudges for entrance.

I don't think twice. I act the wanton, and swing my legs up behind his back, opening myself to his full length. He accepts my unspoken invitation by filling me until he can go no further, with him a tight fit.

I love every second. Or is that every inch? His silken length stretching me in all the right places.

I'm thinking it can't get any better when he starts to move, finishing each drive by grinding against my already sensitive bud. In and out, deeper and deeper, until it's as if he's touching my heart and soul.

"I can't wait, I can't." Anything else I've got to say is lost when Zac pulls out almost completely and drives himself home. It's something he repeats until my body shatters, every nerve ending screaming as loudly as I am.

Zac's lips once again claim mine, swallowing the last of my cries. He then adds his own when his body stiffens and he drives into me, out of control, and all mine.

Rather than crush me when he collapses, he falls to one side, taking me with him, his length still buried in my swollen depths. Our eyes lock, the moonlight enough to illuminate that he appears as shocked as I am.

In the end, I can keep quiet no longer. "Is that, is that normal?" Despite my knowing that he's no virgin, our coupling still had an out-of-this-world edge to it. Or was that just me?

"No, darling, that was not normal. That was freaking amazing!"

Without a hint of bravado, I have to take his words at face value. There's also no missing him twitching to life again, telling me we've got more *freaking amazing* ahead of us in the moonlight.

Again, he takes me by surprise by reaching out and holding me tight. This means that when he rolls onto his back, I'm straddling his gorgeous body.

"Okay, sweetheart, now it's your turn."

Strange, but an hour earlier and I'd have been hit with performance anxiety at this point. That's not the case now, with my grin as wicked as anything Zac has managed tonight.

ZAC

I'd thought our first time together was mind blowing, but as the days progress, the sex gets even better.

However, I'm no longer calling it that. With Kelly, it's all about making love, of showing her how much she means to me, without words.

It's taking its toll on my work, though. Thanks to Ethan's rule that we have nothing to do with clients, it's made for a lot less sleep than I need.

To make sure I'm well away before the rest of the team arrives at work, I've been setting my alarm for five.

While Tyler knows I'm helping Kelly with the float, he's got no idea how far other things have progressed. The less he, and therefore Ethan, knows about that, the safer my job.

I'm nowhere near in a position to go full time with my furniture restoration gig just yet. That's the other thing suffering because of our liaison, although I've no regrets.

I thought I might get more sleep once Lucky Break finished the renovations at Kelly's family vacation home, but the reverse is true. Now I'm as likely to spend the entire night with Kelly, leaving for work straight from her place.

And because we can't keep our hands off each other, we're getting by on less sleep than we need. It's a little easier for Kelly with her able to grab catnaps during the day.

All that comes to a grinding halt thanks to Lily Finnegan, a Lucky Break client who, unknown to the rest of us, is in a relationship with Tyler.

When Ethan discovered they'd been seeing each other, she'd confronted him about his stupid rule. With that being how Ethan met his wife, he'd been in no position to stop others from doing the same.

On hearing about this change to the rules at the start of lunch the same day, I'd stuffed my sandwich in my mouth and was soon running for my truck.

I take less than five minutes to drive to Kelly's place, where I abandon my truck in the driveway. I no longer need to hide my presence here.

Even better is the porch being private.

Perfect when you want to surprise the lady you love with a little midday rendezvous. As this thought flashes through my mind, my actions slow. Is that how I feel about her?

That I love her? That there's nothing casual about what we've got, despite my being naked just outside her front door? Acknowledging my love for her, both exhilarates and terrifies me. I've never felt this way about a woman. Not even my art teacher all those years ago.

After letting myself in, I find Kelly spread out on the floor of her office, enjoying the sun. That she's down there in her underwear, says she's received no work from the agency.

This, to one side, seeing her luxuriating in the rays like this, fills me with joy. Gone is the woman I'd first made love to, with her confidence growing every time we join. Despite knowing I'm there, she stays right where she is.

"Did you forget your lunch again?" She's said this without opening her eyes, missing that I'm naked.

"No, I forgot this." I drop to my knees and am kissing her soon after. From there, things both speed up and slow down when, between kisses, I explain Ethan's change of heart.

She wrenches her lips from mine as the import of my being here and naked makes itself known. "How long have we got?"

I race to open the front of her bra. "Not enough time to head upstairs." When I slide my fingers into the sides of her panties, she arches her hips, allowing me to remove the delicate item.

It's frantic, it's furious, and it's as spectacular as always. With my heart involved, it's better than ever. The sun warming my back, and Kelly hot beneath me, it's blissful.

Leaving her in the shower, I race back to work, annoyed when I have to turn the wipers on. The plan for the afternoon had been to work on replacing any damaged siding. Now we'll be stuck inside.

And while I've no aversions to being inside—my mind floods with images of Kelly and I earlier—I'd rather it not be with a half dozen sweaty men. As the afternoon progresses, the weather gets worse, along with the tempers of every guy on site.

I'm in a foul mood on leaving. Having to slosh through muddy puddles on the way to my truck does nothing to help. It's as well I have to head home to pick up clean clothes. Kelly doesn't need to deal with me when I'm like this.

My mood doesn't improve when I get home and find the small creek that runs through the middle of the property has broken its banks and gone exploring. Those puddles I'd encountered earlier are nothing compared to the muddy water now inching across the floor of the living room and into my bedroom.

The rain in the mountains must have been torrential to cause flooding this bad. And if the forecast is right for once, it's going to get worse.

Possibly a lot worse.

Rather than stay standing in the middle of the living room cussing and swearing, I march into my bedroom. There, I grab a suitcase off the top of my restored armoire and stuff everything I can inside.

The one pair of shoes to escape the rising flood waters are my dress shoes, which are still in a box on the top shelf. My suit has also survived thanks to being wrapped in plastic. The blasted thing cost me an arm and a leg, so there's no way I'm leaving it to the mercy of the flood.

I'll be the best-dressed homeless person in Coogan's Break.

I know I should also grab any paperwork I can lay my hands on, but with the water now swirling around my knees, I don't want to risk it. Charlie, my old-as-dirt neighbor, often told of the great flood of 1955. While today mightn't be in that league, I'm not mucking about.

The other thing I take after I've jammed my suitcase in the back of my truck is the wooden box containing my late granddad's tools. While worthless on eBay, to me, they're priceless.

My dad sure hadn't wanted them after he'd had to give up work, thanks to his arthritis. And anyway, he was more about power tools than hand tools.

I'm about to go check if Charlie has gotten out when he backs that beat-up Ford truck of his out onto the road. A brief wave in my direction, and he's off, his retriever sitting in the passenger seat and sporting a huge doggy grin.

A couple of seconds later and I'm right behind them. It isn't until I'm down the valley and onto higher ground that I give thought to what I do now. The obvious place to stay is with Kelly, but that's a big step.

While it might be one that I'm ready for, I don't know if Kelly will agree with me. There's one way to find out.

NINE

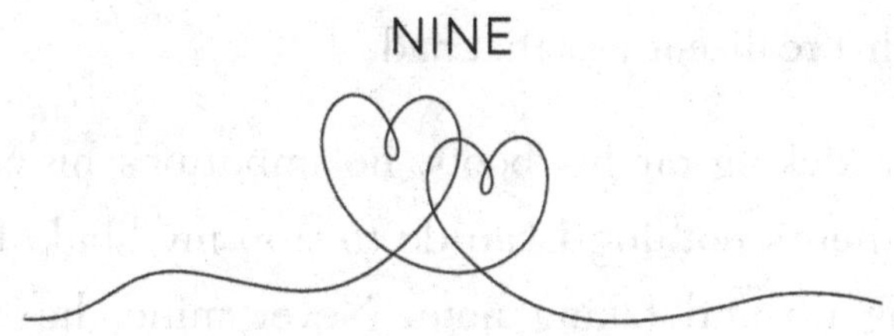

KELLY

While I've been expecting Zac to arrive, I didn't expect him to be carrying a suitcase and a filthy pair of Chucks. And then realization dawns. Haven't I been sitting staring out at the rain all afternoon?

I knew Zac lived in the valley. I just wasn't sure where. That he's been hit by the flooding they've been talking about on the radio is obvious.

"The Chucks can stay on the porch, you and everything else inside."

While he drops the sneakers as instructed, he also drops his suitcase and bends down to unlace his work boots. It's then I see that they and his jeans are soaking wet.

"I didn't realize it was that bad."

After kicking off his boots, he unbuttons his jeans and there's nothing I can do to stop my libido from sitting up and taking note. Never mind, he's just escaped the flooding. Seeing him undress always has this effect on me.

Soon enough, I realize me draping myself all over him is the last thing he needs, and after he steps inside, I peck him. "You go get in the shower, and I'll take care of this lot."

He doesn't argue, telling me he's as cold as he appears, although his shivering could be in response to escaping the flooding. Despite it being summer, the temperatures have dropped thanks to the torrential rain.

It's hard to believe that mere hours earlier, Zac and I were rolling around in the sun on the floor of my office. It's not until he's in the shower and I've tossed his jeans in the wash, and his Chucks in a bucket with some disinfectant, that I realize something.

First, that he'll be living with me, at least until the flood waters recede and he can sort out his place. But, second, and more important to my mind, is that he's chosen to come stay with me while he's homeless.

It tells me a lot, only I'm not sure what it is, and I've come to no conclusions when my phone rings. A glance at the display and I answer it, not waiting for my mom to speak. "I'm okay. The house is fine."

As is often the case, these things sound worse to those in the outside world than to anyone caught up in them.

The next call is from my dad, with him more concerned about practical matters, like is the roof leaking and had I gotten the gutters cleared like he'd asked.

"No leaks." I cross my fingers before adding, "and a guy from that Lucky Break company checked the gutters while he was up on the roof."

My parents appeased. I open the front door and grab Zac's suitcase, grunting with the effort of dragging it inside. I can't blame him for over-packing, though. If it was me, I'd have stuffed everything I could in there, too. And I wouldn't have stopped with one suitcase, either.

The difference would be, I'd have been saving my computer rather than clothes and shoes. Perhaps it's thinking of my computer that has me wandering into my office.

It takes a moment to see what's different about my screen. I've got a new email! Is my time in purgatory over? Dropping into my seat, I'm soon sitting there open-mouthed, flabbergasted and, as that art director from the UK would say, gobsmacked.

It's not from Jason. It isn't even from the head of client services. Rather it's from Caroline Burt, the CEO of Burt's Pet Food. It's not until I've read the email three times that something becomes apparent. Rather than it being to my MC&S email, it's arrived via my website.

There's only one way that could have happened. It's enough to have my hand flying to my mouth. I knew Jason was stupid, but stupid enough to send artwork through to a client with my subtly amended DRAFT watermark still in place?

Apparently so. Soon enough I'm laughing so hard, I'm crying. I'm still wiping tears from my eyes when Zac walks in, a fluffy white towel slung low around his hips.

"What's so funny?"

Unable to answer him through my giggles, I point at the screen, prompting him to bend over and read through the email.

"Oh, that's gold. You know what that means?"

My focus now on how tight his butt is, I don't react.

"Kelly Sanderson, you want to get your eyes off my ass and concentrate for a second?"

His reprimand, full of laughter as it is, does nothing to stop my giggles. It isn't until he puts his hands on either side of my head so he can look me in the eye that I settle somewhat.

"You need to resign, and pronto."

I choke on my last giggle, with him hurrying to pat me on the back to help steady my breathing. "I need to do what!?"

"Resign! Take the woman up on her offer."

Zac has a point. With the non-compete clause in my contract not worth the paper it's written on, there's nothing to stop me working with Burt's Pet Food.

While it doesn't make up for the salary that I'd lose by resigning from MC&S, it'll be enough for me to survive on until word gets around. I don't allow myself to think about it.

While Zac drags his suitcase up to our room, I give Caroline Burt a call as she's requested. Ten minutes after that and I've received a formal offer in writing from her, and tendered my resignation with MC&S.

In his return email Jason is 'devastated', with me not buying it thanks to his letter writing skills being right up there with his creative ones. If I close my eyes, I can see him dancing around his office with whichever intern is at hand.

While part of me is sad to have walked away, another part of me is dancing just as exuberantly as Jason. The difference is that he won't be dancing when he realizes I've poached Burt's Pet Food away from him, and there's nothing he can do about it.

That sorted, I'm soon thundering up the stairs yelling out, "I hope you're not dressed, because I want to celebrate!" While this would often involve champagne or chocolate, it's not my drug of choice these days.

On reaching the bedroom, I find Zac striking a dramatic pose, his eyes alight with lust and laughter. "I'm just a piece of fluff to you, aren't I?"

While he's joking, it's still a question that has me peering at him. Is that what he thinks, subconsciously? My brain then goes where it has no right to. Is he trying to figure out where he stands?

This has me questioning how I feel about him. Then he drags me tight against his hard body and all questions and thoughts scatter to the winds.

I can worry about those later. Much later, if his arousal lasts as long as it always does.

ZAC

As I work on packing my lunch for work, Kelly sorts out our breakfast. It's scary how easily we've fallen into a routine, comfortable both in our skin and around each other.

Despite my worries that Kelly would be resistant to me foisting myself on her thanks to the flooding, nothing could be further from the truth. As well as welcoming me with open arms, she's made Sand 'O' Sun as much my home as hers.

If I'd had any doubts, those vanished the afternoon she'd handed me the TV remote along with a plate of sliders for the big game. Not even my mom spoils me like that.

My cooler next to the backdoor, I join Kelly in the breakfast nook, helping myself to eggs and bacon. "I should be finished early today. We're close to finishing up at the Finnegan job." After downing another mouthful of eggs, I hurry to swallow. "I'll call in at my place on the way home."

Rather than pull me up for referring to her place as *home*, Kelly nods. "I'll be flat out today working on the packaging concepts for that new cat food."

Rather than appear depressed by the thought of working on so mundane a product, Kelly is buzzing, and I love it. I understand how exciting a new project can be. And she sure hadn't been excited about her old job when I first met her.

In some ways, I'm the same with Lucky Break. While I love working with the team, it doesn't float my boat. I come from a family of woodworkers, so to bash in nails for a living is hardly a challenge.

Give me a piece of oak and some fine-grit sandpaper and I can lose myself for hours to the process. And nothing beats seeing the joy on a client's face when I show them whatever I've restored for them.

In the end, the day turns out okay, with Tyler getting me to reinstall the vintage cabinets at the Finnegan place. Once complete, the kitchen could be mistaken as original to the house. That was until you found a state-of-the-art fridge hidden behind pantry doors straight out of the 1930s.

Leaving work at four, I make for my place in the valley. On my last couple of visits, I'd driven straight past, able to see from my truck that the house was still awash. Today is different.

While there's still water in the yard, it's confined to puddles meaning, I can get the insurance assessor in. My never having missed a premium payment, they'll pay out soon enough.

It's on leaning over the fence to talk to Charlie that I start to have doubts.

"What do you mean, they turned you down?"

The old guy shrugs as if to say he doesn't share my surprise, although he soon adds, "I shoulda read the fine print."

It's an offhand comment that has me storming inside my place.

Desperate to find a copy of the policy, I wrench open the bottom drawer of my desk. I then have to jump back to avoid being splashed by the water that fills the solid-wooden drawer to the brim.

Any fine print on the insurance papers is now beyond reading. The same goes for any other documents. Most are now closer to papier mâché than anything admissible in court.

Of course, I don't need a hard copy, not when the insurance company had also emailed one to me. At first glance, my laptop looks to have escaped the flood waters. However, on opening it up and seeing the silt that clogs the keyboard, I know this isn't true.

With me mainly using it for emails, I hadn't even thought to grab it on the day. I thought it'd be okay on the top of the bookcase.

The ruined laptop and paperwork are upsetting, but the desk was granddad's last creation before he died. There isn't a chance I'll let it sit here and rot like my old man.

After yanking all the drawers free and tipping the water out, I drag the carcass out onto the back porch, standing the drawers on end next to it.

The first step is having the desk dry enough to work on. Short of another flood, it'll be dry in a week or two.

My thoughts mired with the idea the insurance company might reject my claim, I drive over to Kelly's place. The one advantage is that I don't have a mortgage. That's thanks to my renovating beat-up thrift store furniture from when I was old enough to hold a scrap of sandpaper.

Even without a mortgage, if my insurance company rejects my claim, it'll be the same as starting from scratch, with me having to fund any repairs myself. It's something I'll need to share with Kelly. While it's okay to stay with her short term, my moving in for the next six months to a year is a different story.

I'm not sure it's one she'll be on board with, and it's way too early for us to be thinking about moving in together. It's an idea that brings me, and my truck, to a standstill, much to the horror of the guy tailgating me. He'd stopped in time, but only just, with me having to inch forward so he can swing around me, before roaring off down the road.

Perhaps I need to consider moving back in with my folks. It doesn't appeal, though. My mom has enough to deal with taking care of my dad without me cluttering up the place. I'd rather be there when she needs my help than be living there twenty-four-seven.

I've made no decisions when I pull into the driveway at Kelly's place. A sense of homecoming washes over me, meaning it'll be that much harder when she tells me I need to find somewhere else.

My other option is to keep quiet until I've spoken to the insurance company. I could be panicking for no reason.

Any thoughts of my insurance claim flee the moment I open the front door and find Kelly waiting for me, with a beer in hand.

However, that's not what catches my eye.

That would be my gorgeous girl wearing a frilly apron in a visage of 1950s domesticity. And I keep thinking this right until she turns and disappears back to the kitchen.

The pink bow of the apron is all that covers her peach of an ass, the ribbons kissing those globes in an invitation to hurry if I'm hungry. Sheesh, I'm ready to eat, alright, licking my lips as I follow her into the kitchen.

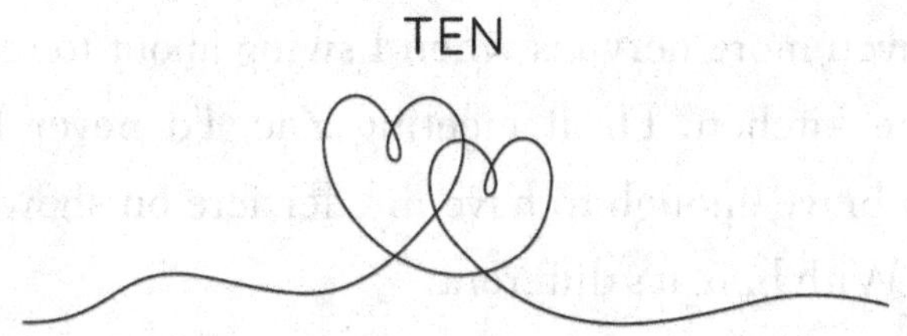

TEN

KELLY

It took me forever to steel my nerve enough to strip off and don the frilly apron. Even more nerve was required to stand there and wait for Zac to open the front door.

Originally part of a zombie Alice in Wonderland Halloween outfit, I'd found the apron when rummaging through the dress-up box at the back of the garage.

There's nothing scary about it tonight.

Unless, of course, you're the one wearing it.

I needn't have worried, with Zac coming close to dropping the beer I'd just handed him.

I'm even more nervous when I swing about to return to the kitchen. Until meeting Zac, I'd never have been brave enough to have my derriere on show like this. With him, it's different.

The way he looks at me gives me the confidence to do things I've only dreamed of in the past. "I hope you're hung..." I don't get to finish my question.

After slamming his beer on the counter, he's spun me around, his lips coming down hard on mine. He holds me tight, his hands crisscrossed over my butt. I'm not going anywhere, and I couldn't be happier.

Is it possible to smile and kiss at the same time? Apparently so, with Zac lifting his head to ask what's funny.

"Nothing. I'm just happy, is all." I wait for him to devour me again, but it doesn't happen. Rather, the light of arousal in his eyes dims somewhat and his hold on me loosens, even if he keeps his hands where they are on my ass.

"Kelly, we need to talk."

I knew I shouldn't have pushed it with this outfit. It was too much, too soon. I should have kept playing it casual, of thinking of him as a friend with benefits rather than...

Actually, I'm not sure what he is to me. What we are. The boundaries I'd constructed to protect myself have crumbled, piece by piece, leaving me open to being hurt yet again.

"I'll, I'll just go get dressed." I then do my best to twist free, but he isn't letting me go without a fight. He once again holds me tight.

"Not unless you want to. Me, I'd rather you stay just as you are."

He follows this up by kissing my forehead, which goes some way to allaying my fears that he's about to dump me.

Can he even dump me when we aren't official?

"I've just been up to my place. It's not good."

Of all the things I've expected him to say, this isn't it. I'd steeled myself for 'the talk'. The one that starts with, "It's not you, it's me."

In the knowledge I'm not about to be dumped, I relax enough to wrap my arms around behind his back and look up at him. "And?"

His sigh is of the sort that says the weight of the world sits upon his shoulders. "I was talking to Charlie, my neighbor." He stops again, and my breathing slows. "His insurance company refused to settle his claim. Something to do with the fine print."

Relief floods me, along with a desire to help him solve this problem. I'm all about problem-solving after my years in advertising. Clients didn't come calling when things were going well. "Have you checked your policy?"

He wastes no time going through what he'd found when able to access his place. Of how high the floodwaters were, and the damage caused. If I think about it, everything he owns of any worth sits in the bedroom upstairs.

"Do you back-up to the cloud?"

It's something I'm paranoid about, with my files being my livelihood.

Zac's body slouches against mine, every atom

defeated. "I've been meaning to get around to it, but, yeah, no."

"Did they email you a copy of the policy?"

My insurance company always does. While they might go on about their green credentials, I suspect that rather than wanting to save the planet; they want to save on paper, toner, and postage.

He's still nodding when I wriggle free. "If your email is web-based, we can access it from my machine." I'm almost in my office when Zac stops me.

"Hang on a second, sweetheart. I don't want all the neighbors seeing my woman like that."

I'm still coming to terms with him calling me his woman when he removes his jacket and drapes it around my shoulders. He's got a point. How often had I been at my desk when Mary waved to me while out on her morning walk?

It doesn't take long to log into his web mail and find the email from the insurance company. Soon enough I've printed out the attachment on tabloid size paper and we're in the dining nook skim-reading it.

If not for my printer being able to print the policy out nice and big, we'd have missed the addendum for sure. Doubtless why it's tucked away at the end of the policy, when most people will have glazed over.

Zac is the first to react.

"What the hell is a negligence clause?"

Busy as I am trying not to cuss, only a few words from the wordy legalese jump out at me. "If the insured fails to take reasonable steps to prevent or mitigate flood damage, any resulting losses will not be covered."

Zac has no trouble cussing, and I can't blame him when the import of the nasty little addition makes itself clear.

"But how was I supposed to take reasonable steps? There weren't even any warnings!" He then rakes his fingers through his hair, a deep growl in the back of his throat.

According to the local radio station, the intensity of the flash flood had even taken the authorities by surprise. Short of him having his place constantly surrounded by a six-foot wall of sandbags, there was never a chance of his insurance company paying out. "Those, those ..."

Next to me, Zac is now bent double, bouncing his forehead off the table, interspersing each thud with a cuss word, and an occasional 'sorry' for his language.

I can't blame him for swearing. I would, too, if not for mom going on about it not being how a young lady talked. "This makes my blood boil."

While not illegal, the addendum is sure immoral. It's also borderline shady. Busy as I've been fuming on his behalf, it takes a little longer than it should for things to slot into place.

First off, Zac is homeless.

Second, he's likely to remain so for the foreseeable future.

Much as I want to suggest he move in with me full-time, I can't get the words out. It doesn't matter that he's as good as living here these days, and that his boss will no longer fire him for it.

It's too soon, isn't it?

More upsetting is that he mightn't want to stay, other than casually.

ZAC

How could I have been so stupid? Instead, I'd let that insurance agent pressure me into signing the policy before I'd read it all the way through.

Much as Kelly is fuming that the insurance company had buried the addendum, if I'd taken the time to read all the fine print, I would have seen it.

Wouldn't I? Truth be told, I hadn't even made it halfway through all those clauses, never mind to the extra bits at the very end.

My forehead still resting on the printout, even up close and enlarged, the font is still at the 'nothing to see here, move along' end of the spectrum. Add in that it's in a soft gray, rather than a more easily read black, and maybe I was never meant to read it?

Either way, I'm screwed.

And while I might be stupid about reading insurance policies, I can read women just fine. Kelly, for instance, is on edge, with nervous energy rolling off her in waves. The only thing I don't know is why.

Could it be she's just realized I need somewhere to stay, and she's not keen on it being here?

Happy to keep screwing me while she needs help with the float, but once that's over, she'll be all, 'Thanks, but no thanks.'

It's then I realize that, but for my interference, she wouldn't even be working on the float.

While it would be easier to keep my head pressed against the worthless policy, I have to face reality soon enough. It's this that has me lifting my head, dread filling me about what will show on Kelly's face.

The last thing I'm expecting is for her to burst out laughing. What she finds so amusing, who knows? Her pointing at me with one hand while stifling her laughter with the other doesn't help, either.

It's not until I stand, and catch my reflection in the mirror above the small table, that I see what it is she's still giggling about. There's no missing that addendum, with it having been transferred to my blasted forehead and left cheek.

When I lean in, I can even read the slippery little clause I'd missed when I signed on the dotted line all those years back.

Maybe I should leave it there like a temporary tattoo?

A reminder not to move too fast. And then I blow it by ignoring this sage piece of advice to myself.

"Kelly, I'll just grab my things and head on over to my folks' place." I haven't given myself time to think about it. I haven't wanted to.

Kelly's laughter is snuffed out in a heartbeat. The light in her eyes is extinguished as in a blink, replaced instead by soul-numbing pain. Shouldn't she be relieved rather than hurt?

Could it be I've misread the fine print yet again? I'm in uncharted territory here. I've never stuck around long enough to get this close to a woman. Hell, I've even admitted to myself that what I feel for her might be love.

The only woman I've said that to, and meant it, was my mom.

While I've said it on plenty of other occasions, it's come all too easily and without my heart being involved. I've said it because it was expected, not because I believed it for a second.

I'm out in the hallway before Kelly reacts, and again she takes me by surprise.

"Like heck, you are!" she yells out. She's beside me a second later, adorable in that apron, my jacket over the top. She's also furious, her eyes flashing. "You are not leaving here until we finish that blasted float."

After stabbing me in the chest with her finger, she then stabs her finger toward the garage beneath us. "You got me into it. You can see it out."

I don't know what to make of this? Does she expect me in her bed tonight, or is that part of our relationship done with? Am I just sticking around to help with construction?

I've come to no conclusions when she shrugs out of my jacket and hands it back to me.

She then turns on her heel and marches back into the kitchen, flashing her ass with every swish of those ribbons. This, more than anything she could have said, tells me where I'll be sleeping tonight.

Is this just physical for her? The irony that I've left many a woman struggling with this exact question isn't lost on me.

· · ·

I wake the next morning feeling more confused than ever after our gentle love-making. I'm climbing into my truck when the old girl from next door pops up out of nowhere.

Kelly then opens the central garage door, with the old lady's gaze swiveling between us, a knowing glint in her eye. It's not there for long.

"Mary, Zac's house got flooded, so he's sleeping in the bunk room until we finish the float. That's right, isn't it Zac?"

I can either agree with the woman who'd spent half the night screaming my name, or call her a liar in front of her neighbor. I have to wonder if her wanting to keep it quiet that I'm living here is to avoid the news from getting back to her parents.

Could it be she's ashamed of me, with her family well off, and mine not? Coogan's Break could be so clicky. Even when the residents in question were part-timers.

At this stage, I've left responding long enough. By now, Kelly will be as hot and bothered as she had been not fifteen minutes earlier when I was sucking on her nipples like a starving man.

"That's right. As soon as we finish the float, I'll be off to stay with my folks north of town." After an obvious check of my watch, I add, "Better get going if I want to keep my day job."

I've backed out onto the street and am ready to drive off, when I call out, "Kelly, I'll see you later. We can carry on where we left off."

While the neighbor will doubtless take this comment as referring to the building of the float, the color in Kelly's cheeks says she's received my filthy promise, loud and clear.

When I run my tongue across my bottom lip, there's no missing her squeezing her thighs together. Good, because I want her wanting me as much as I want her.

Maybe even to love me?

ELEVEN

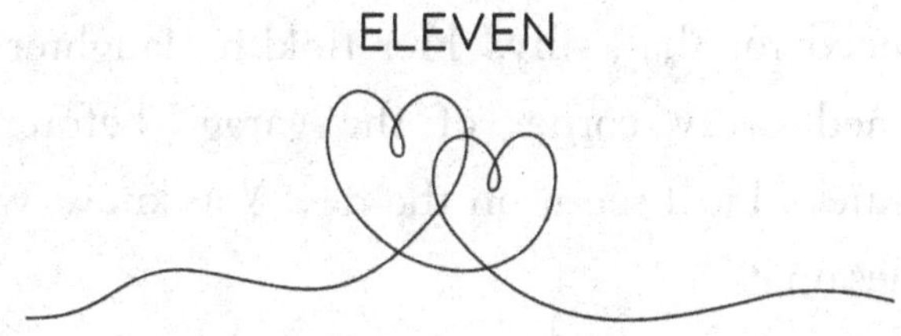

KELLY

Zac Thomas is pure evil, leaving me wet with need like this, and with no way of dealing with it. At least not without telling Mary I'm feeling unwell and sending her on her way.

Instead, I have to kill twenty minutes chatting to her about the float and going through our progress in painstaking detail. It wouldn't be the first time I'd had to convince a client to leave their comfort zone.

"Oh Kelly, it's wonderful! Barry will adore it."

I keep forgetting about her husband, having not seen him since the infamous meatball debacle as Zac refers to it. "We'll send you photos after we've assembled everything over at the lock-up."

"No need for that, silly." Her tinkling laughter has lightened every corner of the garage before she continues. "He'll see it on the day. You know, when he rides on it."

While loath to find out what she means, I also hate being taken by surprise at the eleventh hour. And this surprise sounds like it'll be a doozy.

I have to clear my throat before I squeak out, "Rides on it?"

Mary, having left, I waste no time in racing to the hardware store. Zac will need to reinforce that rocket if we're to avoid Barry boldly going where no man has gone before.

Maybe if Mr. Miller was nicer to the neighborhood kids, he wouldn't need to be on there at all. The thought of the old guy sitting up there all alone isn't a happy one, but there's nothing I can do about that.

I can't wait to see the expression on Zac's face when

he hears about it. His ability to laugh at the most ludicrous situations is one thing I love about him.

I love him? But, I can't. Not having known him for a little over a month. "Oh, what have you done?"

With no answer forthcoming, I carry on to the hardware store, my mind awhirl with what it all means. Another bout of heartbreak for me seems the most likely outcome.

With thoughts of my newfound love for Zac filling my head, I'm in a daze when I walk through the main doors at Tremaine Hardware. I turn right and head for the lumberyard as on previous trips with Zac, not looking where I'm going.

I'm wondering how I'm supposed to keep my feelings to myself, to avoid being hurt, when I see him. Unfortunately, he's not alone. He's chatting to a woman who is everything I'm not.

Tall, tanned, stunning, and wearing a skimpy tank top and cut-off denim shorts that I'd never get away with, let alone into. Her long brunette hair pulled up into a tight ponytail, only adds to her overall height, leaving me Hobbit-like in comparison.

When this goddess then reaches out and places her hand over Zac's heart, I miss a step.

There's nothing I can do to avoid the teetering pile of watering cans in the middle of the wide front aisle. I send the brightly colored cans in all directions. In my favor is that they're plastic rather than metal.

Despite the muted bongs as they bounce off the concrete floor, I don't hang around to see if Zac has seen me. After stumbling into a side aisle, I flee. I'm just as quick to leave the store, and even the parking lot.

There's no way I'm driving home. If I go home, he'll likely be there so he can spin me some BS about her meaning nothing to him, and that they're old news.

She didn't look like old news to me. She looked like the latest glossy magazine.

After parking down at the beach, I wander along the wide expanse of sand, all while ignoring a half dozen phone calls. What starts out as heartache soon turns into anger, although I'm as angry with myself as I am with Zac.

And why am I even surprised?

A guy as hot as him would never stick with someone like me. Not when there are women on offer like the one that I'd seen at the hardware store.

They went together. She was what people expected when they saw a guy like Zac. Not me. As we say in advertising, I'm all wrong for his brand.

All wrong for him.

I've completed six lengths of the beach when an email from the President of MC&S pings up on my phone. If not for its arrival, I might have continued walking until I collapsed in the sand and gave into my tears.

Now, instead of being lovesick, I'm sick to my stomach with worry that the email is to tell me I'm being sued for poaching Burt's Pet Food. And while I can fight it, the ensuing court case would be drawn out and expensive.

However, his email is about nothing of the sort, although I have to read it twice to get the full import of what he's offering.

In a nutshell, he wants me to come back. He's even offering me my dream job, that of Executive Creative Director.

I drop to the sand with a bump, memories of my time with the agency rushing back. The impossible deadlines, the politics. Of never feeling like I belonged. It doesn't take much reflection to realize I'd been miserable.

And for a long time, too. Can I face that way of life again?

"Hah, life?!" I hadn't had a life thanks to the hours I'd worked. My friend circle restricted to anyone at work who wasn't avoiding me, after I'd received the kiss of death from Jason.

And yet, isn't the ECD job what I've been working toward all these years? What I've been striving for? I'd be nuts to turn it down.

This has me checking the email from Brian Mackey again. While he's offered me my dream job, there's nothing in there about what Jason is up to. I snort out in horrified laughter at the idea of the jerk having to report to me.

The opportunity for payback is tempting. But tempting enough to leave Coogan's Break where I've felt like I belong?

And then I remember Zac, and that woman, at the hardware store. The thought of running into them whenever I'm out and about is enough to have stomach acid clawing at my throat.

How dare he take advantage of my good nature when he's seeing someone else? My emotions in disarray, my reply to the company president's email is brief, almost rude.

> Thanks for the offer.
> Before I take it further,
> what happened to Jason?

I'd never have replied to him this way in the past, not even bothering with kind regards as I always would. But that was before he'd promoted the less-qualified Jason over me, putting the brakes on my career.

The injustice of this, coupled with finding out Zac is cheating on me, and I'm too angry to respond rationally. The closer I get to home, the angrier I am.

Angry enough that I don't slow when I see Zac's truck in the driveway, screeching to a halt next to it. As I get out of my car, I mutter to myself, practicing what I'll say to him.

However, the moment I open the front door, I lose the ability to speak. While Zac sits on the bottom step of the staircase, the woman I'd seen him with earlier leans against the newel post.

And poke me in the eye with a stick if she isn't even more stunning up close.

I'd race upstairs and lock myself in our—make that my—bedroom, but with Zac blocking my escape route, that's not possible. Instead, I'm rooted to the spot, my breathing shallow, my heart faltering in my chest.

Zac gets to his feet, running his hands down the front of his jeans. "Kelly, it's not what it looks like. I'd like you to meet Audrey, my sister."

I'm deciding whether to believe this, when a man appears from the kitchen, who is everything Zac isn't. The guy looks like he took a wrong turn at an accountancy conference.

"And I'm Clive, her husband." As if sensing my incredulity, he shrugs, as if to say he can't believe he snared a woman that gorgeous, either.

If I still had doubts, Audrey then holds her hand up,

flashing a stunning solitaire on her slender ring finger.

Okay, now I'm lost for words. Not only is Zac not cheating on me, there's also the lure of my dream job to consider. It would be nice if I could have it all, but I can't.

If I knew Zac loved me in return, it would be a simple decision. But, am I willing to say no to the job of a lifetime for a man who's here for a good time, and not for a long time?

ZAC

Kelly appears stunned, just as I'd been when I ran into my older sister at the hardware store. I hadn't seen her in years. Ever since my folks caught her in their bed half-naked and drinking beer with a guy who was covered in tats.

The old man had blown a gasket and told her to get up and make herself decent. When she hadn't jumped to do his bidding, instead snuggling up to her boyfriend, dad lost it.

He'd called her every name under the sun while chucking all her stuff out in the front yard.

I think he's come to regret it over the years, but with Audrey disappearing without trace, we'd all given up hope of ever seeing her again. It had taken her coming up to me and putting her hand on my chest like she used to when we were little for me to recognize her.

She's changed. We've all changed. Most of all, my dad, who I know, will be pleased to see her, although Audrey is skeptical.

"Zac, I'm back here to see you, not him. Dad told me what he thought of me that day. You don't forget something like that in a hurry."

And I can't blame her. Dad called her some awful names the day she left.

Seeing her again has brought one thing home to me, though. I need to tell Kelly how I feel about her. I don't want to risk losing her because I'm too scared to say something.

Much as I've had fun with my carefree life, I haven't looked at another woman since first laying eyes on her. I don't want to look. I have no desire to look. She's everything I've always sought in a woman, only I hadn't known it.

Eventually, Kelly finds her voice. "You're his sister?"

Audrey unhooks herself from the newel post and steps forward, holding out her hand, ready to shake on it. "I am. I got all the good looks."

On hearing my big sister spouting the line she'd used to when we were kids, my heart lurches. I've missed her so much. I'm not letting her away with that, though. Never have, never will.

"In your freaking dreams, Aud."

And just as when we were kids, Audrey gives as good as she gets. "You're shorter than me!"

I snort before firing back. "Yeah, but that's because your boots have three-inch heels."

Clive, who I've just met, now stands next to Kelly, and I can't help but notice the pair could pass for brother and sister. Funny how Audrey and I have a similar taste in partners.

Even funnier is them watching Aud and me sparring like it's a tennis match, their eyes swinging from side-to-side as insults are traded. It's the flash of Clive's wedding ring that has me realizing what I want.

But am I ready for that? Ready to settle down?

"You'd be a fool if you think twice about it."

This observation from Audrey has us all turning to look at her, wondering what she's talking about. Certainly, it's nothing to do with our back and forth. Then I see the tiniest tilt of her head in Kelly's direction, and I catch on.

I have to hope Kelly hasn't, because it's a big step and it's not one I'm sure I'm ready to make.

"Audrey, Clive, you're welcome to stay here while you're in town." Kelly gestures to the staircase before adding, "There are plenty of spare rooms."

My sister's relief is palpable with her having just told me they were having trouble finding accommodation. While I've told her dad is ready for a reconciliation, it's another thing to front up and hope you can stay.

Far better if she and Clive stay here and call out to see the folks to check the waters first. That way, if things go to hell, they won't be stuck having to pack up and leave on the spot. Even then, it might be better if they stay here, as our childhood home is nowhere near as large as Sand 'O' Sun.

Clive is the first to acknowledge Kelly's invite. "Thanks. That'd be great."

. . .

Catching up with my sister over dinner is everything I could have hoped for. She'd left home when I was just seventeen, and there wasn't a day I didn't think about her.

To hear she and Clive are living beachfront in Hawaii, that she's got a great job in IT and is happier than ever, and I'm more than jealous.

Hell, it's more than I've got, with my job enough for now, and my relationship with Kelly too early to call.

However, on climbing into bed next to Kelly, it sure feels right. I've claimed her lips in a searing kiss when I hear, "Night, John Boy!" from the bedroom at the very back of the house.

Hah, I'd forgotten that stupid tradition, although I soon return with, "Night, Mary Ellen!".

Next to me, Kelly is laughing, although I suspect it's at me rather than the old family joke. Few people remember Walton's Mountain these days, with this tradition one we'd inherited from our parents.

The moment I reach over and turn out the lights, Kelly's laughter softens, unlike parts of me.

. . .

Breakfast the following morning is a raucous affair, with Audrey and me sparring as we always used to, much to our mom's annoyance. It was the same at every meal, with her beseeching us to be quiet and eat.

Even Clive joins in now and then. Meanwhile, Kelly keeps quiet, watching us all with what I suspect is envy. This strikes me as weird, because she's told me enough about the extended family gatherings held at Sand 'O' Sun to know they're anything but subdued.

This also has me remembering our teasing over breakfast some mornings. Of course, those interactions had always had a healthy dollop of innuendo and flirting in the mix. Not something we can indulge in with guests on hand.

Yet again, I wonder if Kelly is as into me as I'm into her, setting aside our physical wants and needs. Hah, as if I could. The merest glance in her direction has me remembering how she'd looked earlier spread out on the bed, her secrets open to my gaze. Open to me.

Next to me, Audrey bursts out laughing for no apparent reason. The way she then waggles her eyebrows lets me know my ogling of Kelly hasn't gone unnoticed.

At least not by my sister and her husband.

Kelly could be taken as oblivious, if not for the high color in her cheeks. A color I'd seen not half-an-hour earlier.

"I need to get going to work." I'm on my feet while it's still possible for me to stand up straight. As fast as I've left the kitchen, grabbing my cooler on the way, Kelly is still there to see me off.

I lean back inside the front door and give her a chaste peck. "If we didn't have guests, I'd hike you up on the porch railing and take you right now. And to hell with the neighbors."

I then laugh at her frustration. Good, I won't be alone is spending the morning longing for completion.

TWELVE

KELLY

It takes twenty minutes in the shower before I'm in any fit state to rejoin our guests. Time spent lathering myself more than was necessary, and something I held Zac responsible for.

It was while dressing that my thoughts strayed to whether our relationship was all just physical for him. Seeing him with Audrey yesterday had been horrible, letting me know how I'll feel when Zac leaves me for someone else.

As he's bound to. I can't kid myself on that front. Is he staying here because of the flood, or because he wants to? That it's because of the flood makes more sense to me.

What are the chances that as soon as he can move back home, he'll be gone with as much speed as that flood had arrived? Not a happy thought with which to start my working day.

But not just yet. "Audrey, Clive, are you ready?" There wasn't a chance I was letting them walk into town to pick up their rental car, which they'd been talking about over breakfast.

Zac had offered, but with him ready to leave before the rental car company was even open, I said I'd take them instead. With them having fussed with their appearance in readiness to meet the folks, they'll not want to be all hot and sweaty when they do so.

It's not until we're on our way into town, with Clive in the back and Audrey riding shotgun, that the pair start their interrogation.

Not since my first interview at MC&S have I been this under the gun, with the pair taking it in turns to fire questions at me. How long have we been dating? How did we meet? Where did I see it going?

I'm doing my best to foist them off with half-truths when Audrey goes in for the kill. "It must be serious for you to be living together."

My response to this is garbled and full of the flood, and just helping and other pathetic excuses. I then glance to the side and see Audrey is grinning. I've had no one tease me like this since I was a kid, leaving me unsure how to deal with it.

In the end, she takes pity on me. "It's okay Kelly, I'm just surprised. Zac was a heartbreaker before I left. I'm not sure my brother is the settling down kind. And yet ..."

It's then all I can do not to slam on the brakes, grab her by the shirtfront and grill her on what comes next. It'll be more than I know. However, Audrey remains close lipped, not offering any other insights.

After she and Clive get out at the rental place, Audrey leans back into the car. "Kelly, just be careful, okay?"

Of all the things I've been expecting, Audrey warning me to be careful around her brother, wasn't one of them. Isn't she supposed to be telling me that if I hurt her brother, she'll hurt me?

. . .

Back at the house, I check to see if Brian Mackey has replied to my blunt email. Was Jason still working at MC&S, or had karma bitten him on the ass as he deserved? Until I know, I'd be a fool to even consider the ECD job.

Several hours later and I've still not heard from the president, or even from one of his minions. This has me firing off emails to anyone I'm still in touch with at the agency to see if they know anything. The only response is crickets.

I can't chase it up with Brian Mackey, because if I do, I'll be showing I'm interested in the job. Never a good idea when negotiating with a man as cut-throat as him.

I've no sooner thought this, than I'm questioning if I'm even still interested in the job. Or is this more about retribution? Of knowing Jason had found out first-hand what it's like to be cast aside?

Or could my being interested in the job be because I'd worked toward it over the years? You can't just drop a long-held goal like that. At least, I can't. Of course, that was before I had a significant other in my life, if I can call Zac that?

And that's my problem. I have no clue what I've got with him. Is it enough to turn down the ECD job if Jason has moved on or, better yet, been fired?

That's a question only Zac can answer.

Unable to decide if I hadn't shot myself in the foot with my initial email, I park it for later. Maybe if I dither long enough, the universe will decide for me as it had in the past.

It wouldn't be the first time Brian Mackey had left someone hanging to soften them up. Deciding there's nothing more I can do about it, I turn to the latest brief from Caroline Burt.

Still, as I work away on updating the design of her company website, my mind keeps straying to what it would be like to be ECD. Much as I'm enjoying the minor projects Caroline is sending my way, they're not enough to survive on.

Nor can I put my freelancing on hold while I wait to hear more from MC&S.

If I end up turning down the ECD job, I'll need more clients than just Caroline. Another four or five at least, and that'll be no simple task. Tough enough to have me concentrating on smashing out the website designs for her and firing them through early.

This out of the way, I double-check everything on my freelance website. I want it to be as sharp as possible. The last thing I need is to approach new clients, and then have them spot a typo, low-res image, or for there to be a broken link.

So engrossed am I that I almost miss my phone buzzing away deep inside my purse. And as long as I take to unearth it, I come close to missing the call. It's Zac with the timber of his voice and the background soundtrack telling me I'm on speaker phone. Note to self, no sexy talk.

"Hey Kel, Audrey, and Clive are here after catching up with the folks. It went well." He pauses in response to someone talking in the background before carrying on. "They're treating mom and dad to a dinner out tonight and want us to join them."

While my brain is screaming NOOOOOOOO at the idea of meeting Zac's parents, my mouth misses the memo.

"That sounds lovely. What time?"

"Maddigan's at seven." There's no missing the surprise in Zac's response to my ready acceptance of the invitation. Was he expecting me to say no, thus allowing him to get out of it, too? Well, it's a bit late now, isn't it?

"Okay, I'll see you later." I'm about to end the call when I think of something.

"Did you grab anything nice to wear when you were clearing out your place?"

While I've doubtless got something I can wear to a place as ritzy as Maddigan's, I'm not sure Zac does.

He laughs before answering. "I did, but damned if I thought I'd have to wear a suit short of someone kicking the bucket. Can you grab it out of my suitcase and hang it up? I don't want to go to Maddigan's looking like trash."

It's then that I realize anything of mine will be in a similar condition. I haven't left the house much in all the months I've been here. Who knew how wrinkled anything formal of mine would be?

While my kind-hearted neighbor might be brilliant at watering plants and drinking all my champagne, she'd told me she wasn't great at packing. And thus, it proves true as I rummage through the strange assortment that she'd sent north for me.

It turns out she'd only packed one evening dress, a Jersey knit number in a dark, moody bronze. It's also one I've never been brave enough to wear.

Bought online, on a whim and never to see the light of day after I'd opened the package. The neckline plunges, meaning I'll need to be careful I'm to avoid giving Zac's mom and dad an eyeful.

Meeting them for the first time will be enough of an ordeal. Double when I don't even know how to describe what Zac and I have. It's enough to have me gasping as much as the steamer my neighbor thought to pack as I work out any wrinkles in Zac's suit and my dress.

ZAC

She should have given me some warning. Not opened the door wearing a dress that has my cock twitching in readiness. "I hope you've got a coat to go over that."

Her worries already clear, she plucks at the dress. "Oh no, what's wrong with it?"

"Nothing at all!" A quick check of my watch and I back up, slamming the door shut behind me.

I step forward, my hands swishing the front of the slinky wrap dress to the sides like curtains. My hands slide deep inside her panties a second later. Now, my cock's no longer twitching, it's on its way to being rock hard. Painfully so.

"Zac, we can't. What about the others? They'll be here soon, won't they?"

In answer, I step forward, pressing her into the wall. While my lips move across hers, I bury my fingers in her curls, reveling in how wet she is. I break the kiss long enough to whisper, "They're going to dinner in what they were wearing earlier."

Her moan is enough to have me cradling her ass under the dress, lifting her and holding her heat against my cock where it strains against my jeans. "I don't care if we're late. I want you so bad, it hurts."

Her frantic nodding is all the answer I need, lifting her higher and being rewarded when she wraps her legs tight around my hips. It's a close-run thing, but I get us up the stairs and into the bedroom before either of us loses it.

Her dress is perfect for what I've got in mind, a simple tug on the belt enough to have her laid bare. While I'm all for tossing the dress to one side, Kelly won't hear of it.

"Don't you dare."

She then rushes to hang it up before turning to face me, her cheeks flushed, her eyes downcast. There's nothing shy about the moisture showing through her sheer panties. Even if I hadn't felt her dampness earlier, I'd know she's ready for me.

I strip like my clothes are on fire, not caring where I toss anything. Next to me, Kelly unclips her bra and puts it on the club chair beside the dresser. She's just shimmied out of her panties when I grab them off her.

A couple of steps later and I slide them into the top pocket of my suit jacket, the slash of pink looking like a decorative handkerchief.

The difference being that we'll know she's sitting next to me at dinner not wearing any panties. To survive, I'll have to take the edge off.

I'm as quick to rejoin her, pressing her back onto the bed. Knowing that she's ready for me, rather than waste time with foreplay, I line myself up and, without pause, slide into her heated embrace.

I don't stop until I can go no further, withdrawing almost all the way before slamming back home again. Her guttural moan is all the encouragement I need, driving home again and again until her keening fills the room and I explode soon after.

Another glance at my watch and her panties poking out of my jacket pocket, and I stay right where I am.

I'll never last the evening without a lot more loving.

While my folks won't notice my arousal, my eagle-eyed sister will, with her warped sense of humor, telling me she'd never let me get away with it.

Despite my best efforts, five minutes after being seated at the large table in the middle of the restaurant, I know it's been a hopeless exercise. Next to me, Kelly's body is pliable in response to our recent lovemaking. In contrast, her wild curls are even wilder and her lips plump.

Of some relief, is that her earlier nerves at meeting my parents are nowhere to be seen. I've never seen her so relaxed, something I'll have to remember for the next time I see her on edge.

"Everything alright, brother?" This query from Audrey has me twisting toward her, in time for her to blow pepper in my direction. As fast as she's been, I've moved even faster.

How could I have forgotten that my big sister can read me like a book? There isn't a chance I can use my pocket handkerchief to blow my nose, although there's no forgetting it's there. Kelly's special scent is a reminder of how she'd tasted earlier.

With this going on, keeping up with the conversation is a nightmare. In our favor is that, after a brief chat with Kelly, my folks are now focusing on Clive.

I think this is down to relief that after the no-hopers Audrey dated in her teens, she's settled for someone respectable. Their relief at not having to dine with someone covered in a ton of tattoos is immense.

This has their new son-in-law monopolizing the conversation with tales of growing up in New Orleans, which is where he and Audrey had met. This led on to Audrey and Clive talking of their marriage on a beach in Hawaii.

There's no avoiding the sadness in my mom's eyes at having missed this special event, with even my dad looking downcast. The heartfelt sigh from Kelly is harder to ignore, although I park it for later. Much later.

Despite the focus not being on Kelly and me, dinner can't be over fast enough for us, to the point we politely say no to dessert and leave early. Before that, I give my key to Audrey. "We'll catch you in the morning. It's been a long week. Mom, Dad, we'll be over to see you soon."

Waiting for the elevator to arrive to take us down to the underground parking garage is a nightmare. This is even more so when another couple joins us. So much for working on that fantasy. It's one that'll have to wait.

The same goes for the cab of the truck in the busy parking garage. On arriving home, the old guy from up the road is out walking his dog. It's as if the universe is conspiring against us.

Once inside the front door, Kelly takes off, flashing bits of her I've been dreaming of all night as she flies up the stairs. I'm not far behind her, which means I get to see her diving for the bed, twisting before she lands, then lying there in open invitation.

Her panties tucked into my jacket pocket, I don't bother stripping off altogether, just enough that I can fill her slick depths as I'd dreamed of throughout dinner. Who needs dessert with Kelly in my life?

It's not until we've got it out of our system and removed all our clothes that we lie in each other's arms. Soon enough, her breathing tells me she's asleep.

Still far from sleep, I lie there thinking back on how Audrey and Clive were at dinner. Even with them playing it down in front of my parents, they'd shown their love for each other, which is more than Kelly and I did.

Even my parents were more affectionate.

It's something I continue to think about as sleep claims me. I want what the others have. Much as I'd had fun teasing Kelly by pretending that I wanted to blow my nose after Audrey pulled that pepper stunt, I want more than this.

I want to show my love for her when we're out in public, not just when we're behind closed doors.

THIRTEEN

KELLY

The night after dinner and the fun Zac and I had had when we got home, and I'm late down for breakfast. I'm about to take the last step when I overhear Zac and Audrey chatting in the kitchen.

"Mom gave me the third degree after you and Kelly left. She wanted to know what was up with you two."

I don't dare exhale, let alone move while waiting for Zac to answer. I thought we'd gotten off easy last night. This was especially so after seeing how Zac's mom grilled Clive and Audrey on their destination wedding.

To me, it had sounded blissful. No need to buy a big fluffy dress, no guests, and even no family. Just the man you love next to you. Much as I love my mom and dad to pieces, with my mom involved, it would be sure to be a logistical nightmare.

In the kitchen, Zac groans. "And what did you say?"

Audrey laughs, although it lacks all humor. "Told her I didn't have a clue and to ask you."

She falls silent for a second, no doubt taking the time to examine her younger brother. It was something I'd seen her do often since her arrival.

"Oh priceless. You don't know what's up between you, either. Do you? Not even when it's staring you in the face."

She follows this up with more hollow laughter, leaving me feeling the same. I'm torn. Do I want to hear his answer, or not? Certain I already know what it'll be, I'm thinking about sneaking back to bed when I hear movement upstairs.

Rather than let Clive catch me lurking in the hallway, I step down, tiptoe into my office and ease the door shut. Better than being caught ready to burst into tears.

Unsure of what to do, I sit at my desk and start my computer. With it being Saturday, there's no need. However, I take comfort in the routine. A place where I'm in control, where I feel at ease.

I've done nothing but sit and stare at the screen-saver when I hear the door open behind me. "Are you okay?"

Unable to answer him, I instead nod, before reaching out and clicking my mouse. Upset as I am, I don't take the time to think through my attempt to pretend I'm working. While I'll often work in my pajamas, it's never on a weekend.

A moment later, his hands come to rest on my shoulders. "I take it you heard my sister and me?"

Again, I nod, unable to trust my voice.

"I can't lie to her."

I stiffen under his hands. What does he mean by that?

"And I'm not sure what I'd say, anyway. This is all new to me."

Is he kidding? He's the serial dater, not me. Without moving a muscle, I beat myself up, calling myself out for being an idiot. For my being sucked in by a pretty face and a hot body.

"That's okay. I wouldn't want you to lie." Despite fighting to keep my tone light, it's tricky when you're being strangled by your emotions, and I'm not sure he's believed me. After what feels like a lifetime, he takes his hands away from my shoulders, then leaning over, he kisses me on the side of the neck.

While I've been able to keep my response casual, there's nothing I can do to stop myself from freezing when his lips touch my neck. It would be one thing if I didn't have feelings for him, but that isn't true.

Now all I can do is hope to protect myself from further heartbreak. I went into the relationship knowing this would be the likely outcome, so I can't blame Zac when it happens.

He's not the one at fault. I am. He never promised me more than a good time, and he's shown me that. After composing my face into something that resembles a smile and not a grimace, I stand and face him.

"Why don't you spend the day catching up with your sister and Clive? Once I take a shower, I'm going to work on a direct mail piece to send to local businesses."

Without waiting for his response, I stretch up and peck him on the cheek before fleeing, with any further words stuck in my throat. Let him make of it what he will. If I can get through this with my self-esteem intact, then I'm going for it.

I've not been back at my desk for five minutes when the door to my office opens yet again. "Have fun with your sister." Again, I keep my eyes locked on my screen, pretending to be hard at work.

Truth be told, I'm having trouble focusing. My vision blurred with unshed tears.

"Zac told me you overheard us talking."

My head dips in defeat. The Thomas family is a tenacious bunch, I'll give them that. What is it they want from me?

Audrey crosses the room and looks out the large window to the view beyond. "I've never seen him like this."

If she wasn't right next to me, I could be mistaken for thinking she was talking to herself. "I told you to be careful, but I think I was wrong about that."

Without clarifying what she means, she turns to leave. "I'd better get going. Zac and me promised Clive we'd show him all our childhood haunts."

She's out in the hallway when she leans back into the room. "Kelly, forget what I said, okay? It's not my place to take care of my little brother anymore. Those days are long gone."

A couple more minutes pass before all three call their goodbyes from the hallway and the house settles. I wish I could say the same about myself, with my nerves rattled by what I've discovered, or rather haven't, this morning.

All the half-truths and snatches of conversations have left me unsure where I stand with Zac. All I know is that I need to protect myself, both emotionally and mentally.

Grieving a failed relationship is the last thing I need. Experience tells me that'll kill off my creativity quicker than a head cold, and last a lot longer.

I can't afford to get sick, especially lovesick. This has me longing for fresh air, with the beach at Coogan's Break, the best place for that.

ZAC

With Clive at the wheel of the hire car, we drive aimlessly around Coogan's Break, visiting places we'd loved or loathed as teenagers.

The one location Audrey and I had a mutual hatred of was high school, although for very different reasons.

While I'd hated the academic side of things, she'd hated the name calling and exclusion because of her height. No fun for either of us.

The surf club was as different as you could imagine. Not that either of us surfed. Rather, it was there we found people who were less judgmental.

People who were more prepared to live and let live. Of course, it might have had more to do with the amount of weed smoked than philosophy. Some of our teachers could have benefited from a joint.

Coogan's Break being as small as it is, and with progress having wiped away a lot of our hangout spots, we end up at the folks' place for lunch. We don't arrive empty-handed though, calling in to Skye High Pies on the way and buying up all their cherry pies.

Lunch is a simple affair, but tasty none the less, with mom having recently bought a bread-maker.

"I've gained two pant sizes since your mom got that darn thing." Dad pats his tummy with his gnarled hands, not in the least unhappy about the weight gain.

And I can't blame him with the smell of fresh baked bread having my mouth watering in anticipation. For sure, BLTs are taken to a whole new level when homemade bread is involved.

After we've all joined in saying grace, mom lifts her head and spears me with one of those knowing looks of hers. "So, Zac, tell me all about Kelly. How did you meet? Is she a local girl? What does she do for a living? Are you two serious?"

Sheesh, I thought I'd gotten off easy last night. I have to give mom an 'A' for efficiency though, with her shooting these questions rapid fire, not giving me time to answer, let along think about an answer.

It's dad who comes to my rescue. "Jean, don't hassle the boy. He'll tell us when he's good and ready."

While it's a reprieve, I know it won't last long. It never does when mom is involved. The feds could learn a thing or two from her.

And, anyway, how am I supposed to respond when I don't know the answers? I can't very well tell her I think I'm Kelly's F*** boy, even if this is what I suspect.

However, I'm man enough to acknowledge that I might have been the one to give her this impression. Casual to a fault, that was me.

Mom takes a small bite of her sandwich, chews on it, and swallows. "She seems like a lovely girl. We were taken with her, weren't we, Patrick?"

Dad nods around a mouthful of BLT, not prepared to stop eating in order to answer.

"Audrey, Clive, you seem to know her a little better. What do you think of her?"

What? She's trying to flip witnesses?

I'm relieved when my sister- and brother-in-law take over the conversation, relieving me of the responsibility of answering my mom's volley of questions. I'm sitting watching the back and forth, when I have a flashback to eight years earlier.

That was the last time I'd introduced a woman to my parents, although they'd been anything but interested back then. "Nineteen is too young to get engaged. You're only babies," was my mom's assertion.

This didn't go down well with me, and especially not with Kirsten. She'd considered herself an adult and didn't appreciate being called a baby. Mom and dad had the right of it though. We were far too young and too stupid to know it was a bad idea.

It had put a strain on my relationship with both my parents and Kirsten. While I'd broken up with her not four weeks later, it had taken longer to reconcile with my folks.

Even now, I don't see them as often as I should, with mom left to endure dad's bad moods when he's in pain thanks to his arthritis. Thankfully, today appears to be one of his good days with him as likely to smile as scowl in pain.

After lunch, I'm all for heading back to Sand 'O' Sun, desperate to see how Kelly is. She was out of sorts when we left, but given I was the reason, I hadn't wanted to stay around and comfort her.

Clive, however, is keen on carrying on. "If it's okay, Audrey promised we could visit a vineyard or two."

I'm about to argue this when I hear Audrey on the phone. "Hey Kelly, just ringing to let you know we'll be home by dinnertime. Uh huh, that's a great idea. Thai okay with you?" She nods before adding. "Great, green chicken curry is my favorite, too."

After this, there seems little point in my arguing for an early return. I shouldn't lose sight of the fact that Audrey and Clive are here on vacation. I'd be an asshole to mess that up for them.

However, as the afternoon progresses, I become more and more desperate to get back to Kelly, to tell her that everything will be okay. To say that I can't commit right now, but that it won't always be like that.

This sees me first through the front door when we arrive home with plastic bags bulging with Thai takeaways. After dumping my two bags on the kitchen counter, I head straight for Kelly's office, surprised to find she's not there.

Hadn't she told me she had a direct mail piece to work on? A quick check of the garage and I can see she's not there either, although there's evidence that she's been busy. The flames streaking the length of the rocket are epic. On closer inspection, I see that she's used spray paint to achieve the effect.

I'm thundering back upstairs soon after, desperate to see the woman I love, even if I can't admit that to myself, or to her.

FOURTEEN

KELLY

After scrubbing myself from head to toe to get rid of any last traces of spray paint, I'm lying on the bed wondering what this evening will bring.

I've come to no decision when Zac bursts in. He doesn't slow until he's launched himself through the air and onto the bed next to me.

I'm still bouncing when he drags me into a tight embrace and kisses me as though his life depends on it. My lips soften under his, as always.

His sigh when he breaks the kiss sounds heartfelt, leaving me wondering what's got him behaving like this. He's a different man from the one who'd left to go sightseeing.

Thanks to the text messages Audrey had sent me, I know they had lunch with their parents, with Zac's sister even promising to stand up for me. Unsure what she'd meant by that, I'd ignored it, replying that I hoped they had a lovely time.

"Come on, sweetheart. If you want more than a sniff of curry puff, you'll need to fight my sister for it."

He then drags me off the bed and onto my feet. Once there, he takes the time to kiss me again, my body responding in a flash. Apparently, it doesn't care one jot that I've got no idea where I stand with Zac, other than tight against him. My attraction is as devastating as ever, perhaps even more so.

Down in the kitchen, every surface is covered with Thai takeaways. "Holy heck, did you guys order the entire menu?"

It sure looks like it, with half-a-dozen overflowing aluminum containers spilling their contents onto the counter. Bowls, cutlery, and napkins sit at the ready next to containers of rice and pools of bright orange oil.

My breathing hitches, not at the mess, but at the memories of that first dinner with Zac rushing back and taking me by surprise. So much has changed since then, especially Zac and me. Whether this is for the good, who knew? I sure don't.

Once our bowls are piled high with steaming Thai food, we settle into the breakfast nook. Thanks to our oily fingers and plates, we aren't going anywhere near the big dining table, with this reserved for holidays.

While conversation is stilted to begin with, we soon move onto how much Audrey and Clive love living in Hawaii. It was while they were there on their honeymoon that they'd decided they wanted to live in paradise full time.

With both of them skilled programmers, they'd even landed jobs before they were due to leave for home. This had blown my theory that Clive was an accountant, even if I still think he looks like one.

"We had to go shopping for interview outfits, because we had nothing with us," laughs out Audrey.

The focus on someone else, I relax as I listen to them working through what they love about island life. They then follow this up with what they miss about living on the mainland.

Audrey wipes her mouth with a napkin, speaking with it still in place, as if to mute her words. "While I love being back in mom and dad's good graces, it's too early to uproot our lives."

After watching Clive nod his support, I turn to find Zac staring at me, an unfamiliar light in his eyes. There's tenderness there for sure. There's also something else that I can't put my finger on. Could it be regret?

I'm having a few of those myself. I'd have expected Brian Mackey to come back to me by now. Had he changed his mind after he got my blunt email?

As I continue locking eyes with Zac, I can't help but wonder if it's not too late to follow up. To, at the very least, apologize for my lack of manners?

I've come to no decisions on climbing into bed, although I take the time to check my phone for any new emails. Still nothing, leaving my life in a limbo of sorts.

This means I can't say anything to Zac. Not until I know what's happening. However, as is often the case when I'm struggling with a decision, my mouth acts of its own accord.

"I got an interesting email from the boss at my old company the other day." Next to me, Zac stills, causing me to add, "Not Jason. The big boss."

"And?"

There's no missing that he's waiting for my answer. His breathing is shallow. I'm almost as frozen before I get up the nerve to answer him.

"Uh, he's offered me a job."

"I thought you said it'd be a chilly day in hell before you stepped foot in that place again?"

Zac's right, I had, but that was before Brian Mackey offered me my dream job. "It's the Executive Creative Director role."

So quiet have my words been, that Zac has to ask me to repeat myself. While he's processing this, I add something I'd never have expected to say in a million years.

"He's offered me Jason's job."

Zac turns and stares at me, aghast. "As in, Jason, the asshole?"

After a snort of nervous laughter, I nod.

"What happened to him?"

It's Zac asking that has me once again worrying about this very thing.

Had Jason's complete lack of talent caught up with him?

Or had management realized he was a misogynistic jerk? Hah, of course not. Not with Brian Mackey belonging to the same club. It was as likely he'd been promoted rather than fired, and that I couldn't cope with.

All round, there were a lot of reasons for me to be nervous about even considering the job.

Zac rolls onto his side to examine me. "If he had to be an asshole to survive in that job, won't you need to be the same?"

Not waiting for my response, he returns to lying on his back, his next words addressed to the ceiling. "I wouldn't have thought you'd go for that."

Of course, if we were talking about the new Kelly, he'd be right. But if we're talking about career Kelly, then he'd be dead wrong.

As sleep claims me, I whisper into the pillow, "I'd be a fool to turn it down," my words quiet enough that Zac won't have heard.

ZAC

Even with Kelly fast asleep in my arms, it's as if a barrier has been erected between us. So, the big city girl is heading back to the big city, leaving the small-town boy right where he belongs.

It's just as well I didn't declare my undying love for her as I'd been planning to. What an idiot.

Women wanted one thing from me. And there was nothing permanent about that. I'm then unable to do anything about the voice inside my head that acerbically says, *"And isn't that how you like it? Casual, with no commitment."*

"Ah, shut up!"

I only know I've said this out loud when Kelly's eyes snap open.

"Sorry, sweetheart, I was talking to myself. Didn't mean to wake you."

I rub her back in calming circles, taking comfort from the action myself. What happened to the Zac Thomas, who could have any woman he fancied?

Here I am, having found the one I want, and now it's my turn to be passed over.

I wouldn't have a clue what the time is when I awake in the night, although the moon high above the skylight says it's nowhere near dawn. Next to me, Kelly is also awake, her breathing giving her away.

I don't care what tomorrow will bring. Right now, I need her.

"Can't sleep?" Much as I want to reach out and make her mine, I'd never do that. And after her telling me about that job last night, I'm unsure of myself.

She sighs before answering. "Yeah, my brain won't shut up."

"You want me to help with that?"

There's enough moonlight for me to see her tentative nod. She's grown so much since we've been together, more than ready to ask for what she wants.

I reach out and splay my hand across her stomach. I love her curves almost as much as the woman herself. She's got more compassion and love in her little finger than any other woman I've dated.

After running my hand down her tummy, I bury my fingers in her curls, and she opens herself to me with yet another sigh. However, this one differs from her earlier response.

As my fingers tweak her pearl, I lean in, my lips close to her shell-like ear. "Let me show you what you mean to me." It's a copout for sure, but try as I might, I can't bring myself to say the words.

If I do, it'll seem as if I'm manipulating her into turning down that job, and I love her too much for that. Soon enough, I bury my fingers deep inside her, finding that other hidden gem, the one that has her gasping in need, whimpering for more.

Then our lovemaking takes on a life of its own. Her hands are all over me, jerking on me, wanting me to fill her, to lose myself, to let her heat scorch my soul.

If our time together will soon be over, I want something to remember her by. I want something that'll last past her return to LA. This has me breaking our kiss.

"Hang on a second, sweetheart." I'm on my feet a second later and over to close the drapes. While both of us enjoy being woken by the sun, it's now that I want the light, not in six hours.

With us protected from any prying eyes, I turn on both bedside lamps, flooding the room with warm light. The other thing that's warm is the room, Kelly only covered by a crisp, white sheet.

Although not for long, with me pulling this back, her skin glowing in welcome. "Tonight, I want to see you. All of you."

I settle between her welcoming thighs, positioning myself to enter how I know she likes it. Even without me touching them, her nipples are puckered and just begging to be sucked on.

Her arching her hips in invitation says they're not the only part of her crying out for attention. As always, she's wet with need and ready for me, and I slide home, jerking my hips to seat myself.

I love how her eyes widen, saying more than words ever could, that she loves the sensation. I have to agree when she tightens her muscles, as if to pull me even deeper.

It's an unspoken request I comply with, lifting her gorgeous legs one at a time and propping them on my shoulders and gaining another inch. My balls are now hard against her body, being slammed every time I drive home.

As we speed up, I don't know where to focus. Her breasts bounce in concert with each thrust. Her eyes are at half-mast, and her lips parted as if to further draw on my hard length.

She arches her neck, the muscles corded, her breasts thrust up in response, her breath coming in pants. Much as I want to let go; I keep a tight rein on my release.

I drive harder, deeper, quicker, determined to imprint myself on my gorgeous girl. Am I being selfish in wanting to ruin her for anyone else? You are damned right I am, because that's what she's done for me.

Her muscles ripple along my length as she arches her hips off the bed and hooks her feet behind my neck. It's as if she's determined to be closer still, and I'll not fight her on it.

Taking all my weight on one elbow, I reach down and squeeze her bud, hard enough that she keens in response. However, it's not a cry of pain. Anything but with her shattering around me a second later.

I'm right behind her, pumping my release into her slick core, never wanting it to end, all the while knowing it has to. My body is now as shattered as my world. I collapse, our bodies touching head to toe.

With my cock still buried, I once again claim her lips, surprised after a minute to taste tears. I'm even more surprised when I realize they're mine.

FIFTEEN

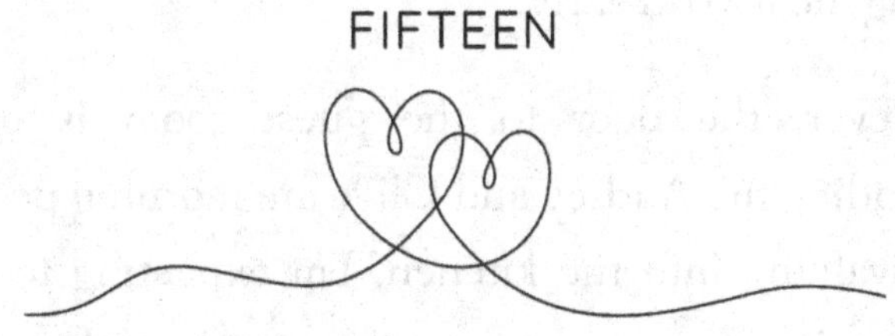

KELLY

The following morning, I wake, stretching my arm out to the side. Rather than a wall of muscle, all I encounter are cool sheets, and the slight dip where Zac had slept.

The door to the master bath open, I know he's not in there. He must have been super quiet this morning. More often than not, while still half asleep, he'll stub his toe, or trip over something. There's no sleeping through his theatrics.

Out of bed, I'm about to head downstairs only wearing a smile when I remember we've got guests. Belted into my toweling robe, I go in search of Zac and the others. That, of course, presupposes our guests are even awake with the angle of the sun telling me it's still early.

However, the door to the guest room is open, reminding me Audrey and Clive are morning people. On walking into the kitchen, I'm expecting to find them with Zac in the breakfast nook. Other than three mugs sitting on the draining board, there are no signs of life.

They must have moved like wraiths not to wake me. Strange, because I'm not a deep sleeper, rather I'm alert to every creak of the old house.

As memories of last night with Zac come back to me, a sad smile curves my lips. There'd been no missing that Zac hadn't enjoyed hearing about my job offer, with his natural exuberance dulled.

The constant was the time we'd spent exploring each other's bodies, with this likely the reason I'd slept through everyone leaving. The difference last night was the bittersweet edge to our lovemaking.

In the cold light of day, I see it for what it was.

A goodbye.

This has me rushing out into the entryway and wrenching open the triangular door to the space beneath the stairs. Zac's suitcase is gone.

He'd known he was leaving when he'd made love to me last night. But why? I haven't said yes to the job.

A hiccup of tears catches in my throat, choking me as surely as the knowledge that whatever I had with Zac, it's over.

Back upstairs, I check the guest room, unsurprised to find the space tidy. If not for the thank you note on the bed, it'd be as if I'd imagined our guests. Our guests? Not anymore, because there is no 'our'.

I don't bother with breakfast, my tummy roiling at the very thought. Instead, I have a quick shower, washing away the last of Zac's unique scent.

Coffee in hand, I'm soon at my desk, for all the good it does. I'm not capable of working, not with my heart in shreds.

Honestly, I thought we had something special, but with neither of us willing to take things further, I guess it was doomed from the start. Of course, I was cagey about committing, not wanting to get hurt, as I had in the past when trying for a guy out of my league.

There was never a chance someone like Zac would tie himself to someone like me. While Audrey was Zac's sister, I just knew there'd be another woman like her waiting in the wings, and who wasn't related.

And yet, I'd soon enough realized there was a lot more to him than a to-die-for body and good looks.

Funny, but the better I got to know him, the less I'd noticed how handsome he was, but even more precious for it. He was just Zac, the man I loved. I should have known better than to fall for a player.

Men like Zac didn't commit, at least not until their mortality came knocking at the door and they experienced the drive to procreate before it was too late. And even then, it wasn't a given they'd tie themselves down.

With tears now running down my face, I ready myself to send another reply to Brian Mackey's earlier email. It's only after swiping my eyes with my sleeve that I see he's emailed me again. Could it be I'm about to hear what happened to Jason?

I hope he's left the company, because with Zac having moved on, it's time for me to do the same.

A skim-read of the email and I know where Jason is, although I'm not sure Sydney is far enough away for me to relax. As well as this snippet, Brian Mackey has repeated his job offer. There's even an attachment to back this up.

He always was an aggressive so-and-so. Rather than a job description as I've expected, it's a firm offer. An actual employment contract, his flamboyant signature taking up most of the last page.

I'd seen firsthand the trouble Zac was in from not having read the fine print on his insurance policy. It isn't a mistake I'll make when dealing with someone like the president of MC&S.

I therefore take my time reading through the contract, stopping now and then for a sip of coffee, or to make notes. And the more I read, the faster my heartbeat.

I'm re-reading the final clause and the lump-sum payment I'll receive on signing when I grab my phone, slamming it back down on the desk.

Brian Mackey is a manipulative SOB. I've seen how he can tie people into knots.

The last thing I need is him drowning me out with glib promises and mansplaining.

Instead, I hit the REPLY button, my fingers poised above the keys, ready to respond. Ten seconds pass, before I snatch my hands away from the keyboard, second guessing myself.

Sure, it's a great job, the best I'll ever get. But, do I want it? Do I want to be at the mercy of that industry again? It wasn't so long ago that my blood ran cold every time I received an email, or even when I didn't.

Like when Jason and the head of client services were ghosting me.

I'm still in stasis when another email arrives, this one from Caroline Burt. The contents are as unexpected as the one from Brian Mackey. The difference here is that this email has my tummy full of butterflies, not boulders.

However, it's also an opportunity that will see me stuck in Coogan's Break with all its memories of my time with Zac. That would destroy me.

This has me re-reading Brian's email with its once in a lifetime offer. I flick back and forth between the two emails, all while adding to my ever-growing list of pros and cons.

In the end, the obvious choice makes itself known to me. I'm still wondering if I'm not "Making the biggest mistake of my life" when I hit REPLY.

My acceptance email sent, I slump back in my ergonomic chair, unsure of what to do next.

But, before starting something new, I need to sort a few things out. The first is that blasted float. With Zac having moved out, I doubt he'll continue helping me with it, too busy searching for my replacement.

I refuse to leave Mary in the lurch. That's not who I am.

Despite my can-do attitude, I'll still have to get the trailer over to Barry's lock-up and find someone else to complete the final assembly. It doesn't matter that the design is mine, I wouldn't know a wrench from a, a ... Whatever some other tool is.

I'm searching for a local building company that isn't Lucky Break Construction, when I see Zac backing into the driveway. This is unexpected. I didn't think

I'd see him again. And why is he backing in? Ready for a quick getaway?

I don't give myself time to think about it, instead rushing for the bathroom so I can splash my face with cold water. There isn't a chance I want him to see I've been crying over him.

ZAC

With Kelly mentally on her way back to LA, she won't want anything to do with the float. The sooner I tow it over to Barry's lock-up, the better.

At least with everything over there, I can get on with the final assembly and avoid the temptation that is Kelly Sanderson. I have to maintain some level of pride.

Sure, leaving before dawn was an asshole move, but once Audrey decided she wanted to commit to staying with Mom and Dad, there was no holding her back. Add in that she and Clive were still on Honolulu time, and they'd been awake since four o'clock.

And while I'd heard them moving around, Kelly, who I'd made love to like it was the last time, had slept on.

Half asleep as I'd been when we left, it was pure luck that had me remembering to grab the key for the lock-up.

When I'd later explained to Ethan about my sister being in town, he'd suggested I take the rest of the week off.

It's the breathing space I need to work out where I'd gone wrong with Kelly, finish the float, and catch up with my sister.

Audrey had been so nervous about her and Clive moving to our folks' place that she'd begged me to spend a couple of days there. And I can't blame her. We both knew how our dad could be.

She wanted me to be on hand to run interference in case the old man changed his mind about welcoming her back into the fold. He could be a crotchety bastard when his arthritis was bad.

It also gave me somewhere to stay until I could organize something else. My preference is something long term to avoid any couch surfing while I fix up my place.

With Kelly accepting that job, it told me that whatever we'd had; it was over. And with her moving back down south, I can't stay at Sand 'O' Sun on my own.

Time for her to return to her real life. That once again, I'd been cast in the role of holiday entertainment by a stuck-up city girl.

I've not had time to engage the park brake on my truck when Kelly is next to my door, and she looks steamed, although why I wouldn't have a clue? I'm only going along with what she's decided.

Mind you, it wouldn't be the first time I'd gotten the wrong end of the stick. While I know my way around a woman's body, what goes on inside their head can be a complete mystery. And Kelly's no different.

However, she was the one who called it quits. Not me.

"Oh, so you've come back, have you?"

She stands rigid with anger, hands on hips, her eyes sparking. And damn it, if it isn't a turn-on. It's a side of her I haven't seen in bed, but if she was to truly let go, wow.

As always, when I'm near her, my cock takes control

of all rational thought, leaving my brain to stutter, "Uh, uh, uh."

Unable to defend myself with her accusations flying thick and fast, I hold my hands up in surrender. She's not done with me, though. Not by a long shot.

"How dare you sneak out in the middle of the night?"

"It wasn't the middle of the night, it was five-thirty." As a defense, it's weak. I had snuck out. I hadn't kissed her awake as I always did, wanting my memory of our last night together to remain unsullied.

When I see her winding up again, I can't stop myself from spitting out, "And anyway, you're a fine one to accuse me of running out. Isn't that what you're doing by accepting that job?"

"What are you talking about? You know nothing of that." While her words lack conviction, her brow is creased with confusion.

"No, of course I don't. Why would I? I'm just a hick from a hick town." My arm thrust out to the side to encompass Coogan's Break; I then carry on. "I don't have time for this crap. Let me grab my tools and the trailer and I'll be out of your hair."

"Like heck, you will. That float is my responsibility, just as much as it is yours."

Despite having just said this, she then points the remote at the garage door, with it lifting in response. Talk about mixed messages. No wonder I have trouble understanding women.

Rather than walk inside and grab my tools, I jump back in my truck, wasting no time shoving it in reverse. However, in my haste to hook-up the trailer and get out of there, I come close to running Kelly over.

It's enough to have my scalp prickling in response to how close I'd come to hurting her. While I might hate that she chose that job over me, I don't hate *her*. Far from it, with my body thrumming with anticipation at being close to her.

I wrench on the park brake and throw myself out of the cab, desperate to see if she's okay. She's frozen behind the tailgate where she'd been when I spotted her at the last second.

Despite having told myself on the way over that I'd keep my distance, I can't help myself. I drag her in for a tight embrace, desperate to prove I'd meant her no harm. Not kissing her goodbye this morning was one of the hardest things I've had to do in a long time.

"I'm sorry, so, so sorry." As I repeat this mantra over and over, I'm no longer sure if I'm sorry about nearly backing over her, or for losing what we had.

Rather than melt against me as she usually would, she stands rigid, her arms tight against her sides. This leaves me feeling as awkward as a pimply-faced teenager at the end of their first date.

Eventually, I realize she won't respond, much less acknowledge my apology. I therefore waste no time in moving her out of the way and getting back in my cab. The sooner I hook-up the trailer and leave, the better. However, this time, I reverse slowly, my nerves still on edge from the near-miss.

In concert with tossing my tools into my toolbox, I fire rejoinders at her. "Hey, if it wasn't for me, you wouldn't have anything to do with the float." I chuck a torque wrench in the general direction of my toolbox before carrying on. "And don't worry, I won't screw up your precious design."

After slamming the toolbox in the back of my truck, I drag the trailer forward until the coupler is over the towbar. Once it's hooked up, I tow it forward so I can load all the extra stuff in the back.

Given the fragile nature of all the bits and pieces Kelly had collected, I'm more careful with them than I had been with my tools.

Of Kelly there's no sign, with her having stormed off in a huff.

"Fine, if that's how you want to be. You go for it!"

With everything loaded and tied down, I lean in and hit the button on the wall, closing the garage door.

It's not until I climb back into my truck that I see Kelly is in the passenger seat, her seatbelt done up, her arms crossed. She's not going anywhere. Other than to the lock-up.

So much for my wanting to keep as far away from her as possible.

SIXTEEN

KELLY

For all the drive to the lock-up takes less than five minutes, it seems like an eternity, stuck in the cab with a seething Zac.

What's he got to be angry about? What did he expect after he moved out this morning before the sparrows had time for their first argument.?

That job will give me the creative freedom I've worked hard for over the years. No more answering to a higher-up and having them question my creative rationale.

On arrival at the lock-up, Zac swings the truck and trailer around in a wide arc, before backing up to the roller door of the end unit. And, for the first time since arriving at my place to grab the float, he looks me in the eye.

"I'll need you to guide me in, Kelly. It's a tight fit and I'll need to drive it in as far as it'll go."

There's no missing the glint in his eye, nor the way he runs his tongue across his bottom lip. The thing that's missing is his usual arousal when he talks to me like this. He's being provocative.

Well, two can play at that game. You don't work in advertising without learning to defend yourself when you need to.

"Hah! It's not THAT big, Zac." I laugh in his face before unclipping my seatbelt and jumping out of the truck. I then lean back in, my breasts shoved in his direction as I hold my hand out for the key to the roller door. "If you try hard enough, I'm sure you'll get it right, for once."

Key in hand, I slam the door on his muttering, worried I've pushed him too far. I don't know if it's because I'd wound him up, but it's only on his third attempt that he's able to back the float into the lock-up.

It's a tight fit, with the trailer separating us, not a bad thing when I fire, "Three tries? That's more than you usually take. Third time's a charm, I guess."

The barrier is nothing, with Zac as wound as tight as he is. He's clambered over the trailer and is next to me before I've even moved. There'll be no escape. Not with me trapped between the float and the wall of the lock-up. He stalks toward me with my retreating apace.

Soon enough, I'm hard up against the back wall, with nowhere else to go. Zac, however, keeps coming, until he's smack bang in front of me. The difference from when he'd stared me down earlier is that his eyes are now dark with arousal.

And blast it if my body doesn't respond. I can't turn off my attraction to him because he's up and moved out. Nor can I change the way I love him.

It'd take months of eating too much ice cream and crying at old movies to help ease the loss of what we had. No matter that I don't know what it was; it was something I'd not had before, and I already missed it.

Zac takes another step in my direction, his body hard against mine, pressing me into the breeze block wall. While it's cold, he's hot. His lips are even hotter when he claims my mouth and my breath.

My body shrieks in desire. At first, I don't see what's different about this kiss. Then it hits me. Gone are all Zac's smooth moves, as if everything has been choreographed in advance. With this kiss I'm getting raw, unadulterated Zac, without that gigolo persona of his getting in the way.

It's devastating in its intensity, cutting through any barriers I'd held on to, hoping to protect myself from potential hurt. With a single kiss, he's laid my soul bare. And yet, hasn't he revealed a side of himself he'd kept hidden, until now?

If not for this, I'd be struggling to get away, rather than tight against him, my tongue tangling with his as I undo the buttons on his jeans. An invisible dam has been broken.

His hands are everywhere, tugging on my clothes, caressing, teasing, making me pliable. My breathing is now as ragged as my self-control, leaving me gasping for more. More of everything, more of Zac.

"Yoo hoo!"

Not even a bucket of iced water would have snuffed out my libido as rapidly. Meanwhile, Zac straightens, struggling to button up his jeans in case Mary Miller ventures to the very back of the lock-up.

While he blocks me from view, I rush to make myself presentable enough to face my elderly neighbor. The one thing I won't be able to hide from her is the arousal that coats my body like oil, leaving me slick with need.

On peeking over Zac's shoulder, I'm reminded the roller door is wide open. It's a good thing Mary interrupted us before I was open to Zac and the world.

"Oh lovely, you're both here." If Mary spots anything different with us, she doesn't comment. At the very least, I've been expecting her to remark on how flushed my face is, and worry if I'm not coming down with something.

I nearly was. With Zac the one responsible. A peek to the side and I'm surprised to see that rather than appearing abashed, his face is flooded with what appears to be relief.

Is it relief that Mary stopped us going any further? Unfortunately, I can't ask, with my elderly neighbor now monopolizing him as he takes her yet again through how the final float will look.

It doesn't matter that the design was mine. She's of the old-school mentality that thinks men know best. She'd get on with Brian Mackey like a house on fire.

It's when Mary asks how Barry will climb aboard the rocket, and what will hold him in place, that I'm okay with being excluded. One look at Zac's face and I realize I'd never gotten around to telling him about this. What with his sister arriving, Brian's job offer, and Zac moving out, it'd slipped my mind.

Worried I'll get the giggles and suggest we can gaffer tape Barry in place, I move away. To the casual observer, I'm checking through items in the trailer, however Zac isn't fooled for a second, giving me a dirty look for abandoning him to his fate.

ZAC

While frustrated to be stuck with the old lady going through everything for what feels like the millionth time, I'm also relieved at the interruption.

I've never let myself go with a woman like that. I'm unsure if Kelly noticed my barricades crashing around my ankles like my jeans had been about to. A quick check in her direction doesn't have her giving much away.

That is until I see her biting her lip. However, I think this has more to do with not laughing at Mary's solutions to keeping Barry on the rocket when it moves.

This assumes we can even get him up there without a block and tackle. He's old and slow, so to expect him to clamber up there unaided has the potential to end in tears.

In the end, I convince Mary that we're on track, with her then tottering back to her car. It's when I'm waving her off to make sure she leaves I spot Barry sitting in the passenger seat. His visage is grim as he stares straight ahead, the epitome of miserable.

Hell's teeth, if we allow him on the float with a face like that, he'll have little kids bursting into tears when he passes by. Not until the ancient Buick has lumbered through the front gates of the industrial park, do I turn to face the lock-up.

After uncoupling the trailer, I inch my truck forward. Of Kelly there's no sign, although she's in there somewhere. After re-entering the unit, I turn and wrench the roller door down.

While I'm unsure what will happen between us, I don't want another interruption like the one we'd just had. The pressure in my balls says they've got to be the color of the sea on a winter's day.

I hear Kelly's laughter before I spot her in the back of the trailer. However, she's not busy getting everything straightened in readiness for assembly.

Rather, she's rolling around on a pile of silver insulation foam and bunting, holding her sides to keep her laughter in check.

"Your, your, your face when she suggested bolting one of their Queen Anne dining chairs to the back of the rocket..."

She's unable to articulate further, her laughter coming out in a series of gasps that make further talk impossible.

"Move over!" When she does so, I flop down next to her, the tail of the trailer tipping more than I'm comfortable with. "That won't be our biggest challenge." I take my time rolling onto my side so I can watch her while I talk. "Remember the other night at dinner, how Barry didn't look happy?"

Rather than return my gaze, she answers with a brief nod. So, that's how it's going to be? Looks like I'm not alone in having regrets. "He was ecstatic that night compared to just now."

"He was here? Why didn't he come in? He's a part of this, too."

I flop onto my back and join her, staring at the metal ceiling high above us. "Yeah, my gut tells me that while his spirit is willing, his body is yelling no."

"Hmmm. I guess it can't be easy being in pain like that."

We fall silent with me busy debating whether to discuss what had happened earlier. The longer the silence lasts, the more awkward it is. To the point I can't stand it any longer. "We'll need a mask."

This grabs her attention, with her turning her head to the side and staring at me as if I've lost my mind. "A mask?"

"Yeah, of Yoda or an alien, or something space-related. There isn't a chance we can have Barry's misery ruining the parade."

"It was that bad?"

I nod before answering her. "Yep. He was not a happy camper."

She again snorts out in laughter, the trailer bucking around to the point the end clanks on the concrete floor. This results in everything sliding down the ramp we've formed.

I don't think twice; I reach out and drag Kelly tight against me, the large tube that forms the hull of the rocket, sliding by right where she'd been. Damn, but that was close. And double damn, but she feels good in my arms.

Why did she have to accept that job?

Could it be because she didn't know how you felt about her?

Despite the undoubted truth of this, while my balls might be blue, they're not big enough to have me fessing up and telling her how I feel.

Could it be a fear of rejection that has me ending relationships before they've run their course, or keeping things so casual that commitment never comes up?

But isn't Kelly worth that risk? I'm getting up the nerve to say something when there comes hammering on the roller door. "What the hell's with this place being like Grand Central Station?"

Kelly struggles to be free of my embrace before inching away and off the trailer, causing the tow bar to crash back to the floor. Rather than wait, she's already on her way to open the door to see who it is.

It's Barry. The last person either of us expected. "Mr. Miller, how can we help?" Much as Kelly has asked, the uneasiness in her voice says she doesn't want to know.

I'm with her on this one. He was here not half-an-hour ago and hadn't bothered getting out of the car. So, why's he back now? With no sign of the Buick, he must be on his own. It's then I spot an Uber parked outside the front gates.

"I don't want to!"

Kelly's brow wrinkles. "You don't want to what?"

The old guy takes a deep breath, as if girding his loins for the challenge ahead. When he then focuses on me, I do likewise. I don't like where this is heading.

"Son, I need your help. Mary wants me to ride up front on the float. Much as I love her, I'm too old for that malarkey."

Busy thinking that I can't altogether blame the old guy, it takes a second for me to focus on some of what he'd just said. "The front of the float?"

He nods while tapping the towbar with his cane. "I ride up front and throw candies at the kids."

"Candies?" Squeaks out Kelly, next to me.

That Barry is unaware of Mary's plan to have him riding the rocket is obvious. I thought it was a big ask for an old guy with failing health. It's also too big for me to be the one who breaks the news to him.

Barry then spears me with a steely gaze. It's one that has me checking over my shoulder, hoping I'm not the target.

No such luck.

"Zachary, you'll need to do it."

I've not thought about how I'll get out of this when I see Kelly in my periphery. After slapping her hand over her mouth, she shoots out the front of the lock-up. A second later and she disappears around the side.

"But what about Mrs. Miller? She'll know it's not you up there."

"I've thought about that, son. The astronaut costume she's picked out for me has a helmet."

I'm still digesting this when I hear a snort of barely contained giggling. Kelly won't be laughing when she finds out she'll be on the rocket with me. I then have trouble concentrating as I imagine her in a sexy space suit.

As her suppressed giggling gets louder, Barry looks around, but unable to see anyone, he shakes his head and presses on. "So, you'll do it?"

"I'll do it alright, and Kelly will be right there with me."

With Barry busy thanking me while pumping my hand, I almost miss the sharp intake of breath from outside. However, there's no missing the coughing fit that follows as the newest member of my 'crew' fights to get herself under control.

His delegation a success, Barry waves to the Uber driver, with the electric vehicle gliding through the front gates and over to stop next to my truck. Rather than Barry getting in, the driver gets out, having popped the trunk.

Soon after, I'm handed an enormous trash bag, with no chance to check the contents before Barry is settled in the back of the Uber. Another cheerful wave, and Kelly's elderly neighbor is on his way home.

I feel no guilt in hoping he's having meatballs for dinner.

SEVENTEEN

KELLY

While I'd laughed when Barry Miller was busy conning Zac into taking his place, it's nothing compared to now. The difference is my laughter is now nervous.

Zac looks so hot in that astronaut costume that I'm having trouble breathing. It fits as though made for him. On closer inspection, I decide it's not a costume, it's the real deal, with the same going for the helmet.

On Zac sliding the gold-colored visor down, I could be mistaken for thinking it's Barry standing in front of me. Except for Zac's overall height and breadth of shoulder, that is.

Okay, and I doubt Barry could rustle up an erection as impressive as the one Zac has on display. Did I mention that the suit was a snug fit?

"I'll wait for you in the truck." Not trusting myself to keep my hands off him any longer, I scuttle out to the truck and slide into the passenger seat.

My heart isn't up to watching Zac wriggle out of that suit. Especially not when he'd had to ditch his jeans to get it on.

Soon enough he joins me, giving me the side-eye for abandoning him. There's nothing I can do to stop my gaze from dropping to his lap, something he catches me doing. Why is it always this hard?

"That's your fault."

My head snaps up, and I stare at him, openmouthed. I said nothing, did I? No, no, I didn't.

"Hah, I wish it was always this easy to see what you were thinking."

A brief shake of his head and he starts the engine. However, on driving out the front gates, rather than head toward Sand 'O' Sun, Zac turns left, toward town.

"Where are we going?"

Now it's Zac's turn to snort. "Sweetheart, if you think I'm riding that rocket alone, you are kidding yourself." He sucks on his bottom lip before carrying on. "And much as I'd like you naked when you do, I doubt the parade organizers would be up for it."

I haven't cobbled together an answer to this when he pulls to a stop outside the only costume hire shop in Coogan's Break.

That's the second time today he's made a throwaway comment that says he's still attracted to me. And let's not forget us coming close to doing the dirty at the lock-up. As if I could.

But in that case, why did he move out? Never once did I say I'd accepted that job. I'm still mulling everything over when he opens my door.

His hand clasping mine, he urges me out of the truck, not giving me the luxury of thinking about it further. Zac leads me over to the front of the costume shop, where he opens the door and nudges me inside.

"I'll trust you to pick the right outfit. Make it silver, make it shiny. Something like my outfit would be good." With his list of demands delivered, he shuts the door in my face and stomps back to his truck.

He then sits unmoving, doubtless in for the long haul. What he doesn't know is that I hate costume shopping, never able to find something I like. Never able to find something nice that fits.

If a costume fits, it'll be one that sees me playing the part of crone, monk, or hippy in what amounts to a sack with a belt. It'll also be something in which I'll look hideous.

On spinning around, determined to have this hell over with, I come close to bumping into a woman. Strange, because there's no missing her in that bright orange tracksuit. It's a bold color for a woman on the wrong side of seventy.

"Hello sweet thing. And how can I help you today?"

While she's talking to me, I'm not the one she's checking out. That would be Zac. When she gushes out, "Oh my, that one could put his slippers under my bed any night," as angry as I am with Zac, I have to agree.

However, I don't have time for this. The less time I

spend in costume hell, the better. "I need something spacey."

"Spacey as in outta space, or stoned?"

Wait? What?! "Oh, outer space, please."

After rubbing her hands together in glee, she spins on the spot and takes off, putting her tracksuit to good use. "Follow me, follow me!"

I do my best, but thanks to the speed at which she'd left, and the higgledy-piggledy nature of the shop, I lose her on the first corner. This is quite the achievement given how bright her outfit is.

I give up trying to find her, instead standing stock-still in the middle of the shop and yelling, "Where are you?" I don't have the patience to play hide-and-seek today.

Despite her calling out, "I'm over here," several times, I'm none the wiser. In the end, she has to come and collect me. After taking my hand in a vice-like grip, she drags me to the very back of the shop, and then into another room.

On spotting a sign above the doorway that says BIG

& BEAUTIFUL, I steel myself to be confronted with the usual plus-size tat.

"This will be wonderful on you!"

I spin around, ready to spit out "NO!" but I can't. I'd never have expected the like in a backwater like Coogan's Break. Even more astonishing is that it looks like it might even fit.

Ten minutes later and I'm out at the truck, gripping a large plastic bag that the lady in the shop had taped shut for me. The one thing that couldn't be crammed in there is the helmet, a smaller version of the one Zac will wear.

The less Zac sees of my 'spacey' outfit before the parade, the better. That's if I don't chicken out and change my mind.

ZAC

Kelly is back at the truck far sooner than I've expected, with me pocketing my phone to avoid her seeing what I've been searching for.

I'm still not sure it's the right choice. But I can't leave things as they are. I'm stupid, but I'm not that stupid.

"I see you got a helmet. Can I see the rest?"

After shoving the haphazardly taped plastic bag in the footwell along with the helmet, Kelly climbs in. "No, you can't."

Well, that was unexpected. "Can you at least tell me about it? Can I assume it's like mine?"

She tsks while shaking her head. "Zac, you know what they say about *assume?*"

She doesn't wait for me to give the usual response, instead huffing out and adding, "You'll have to trust me."

Great! There's a 'NO' if ever I heard one. A couple of days back, and I would have trusted her with my life. Now I'm not so sure. I'd been fool enough to trust we had something together. Then she'd accepted that job in LA.

"Can you at least let me know if it's silver?"

While her smile is slow to start, she's soon grinning like a loon. "Oh, it's silver alright."

. . .

On dropping her back at Sand 'O' Sun, I'm no clearer about what her outfit is, despite peppering her with questions. The more I'd asked, the happier she got, although she'd given nothing away with her answers.

Other than the helmet, for all I know, she's riding the float dressed from head-to-toe in aluminum foil. That and more of the silver gaffer tape like that used to seal the plastic bag from the costume hire place.

Dirty mind that I've got, but on yanking on the park brake, all I can think of is us atop the rocket. My cock jammed against her foiled ass.

Sheesh, what is wrong with you?

She's already grabbed the plastic bag and is about to pick up the helmet when I put my hand out to stop her. "Why don't you leave that with me? It looks the same as mine. I should be able to rig it so we can speak to each other."

That she agrees this will make things easier is confirmed when she drops the helmet back on the floor mat. "I'll see you at the lock-up tomorrow. Mary said she'll give me another key."

My mind is chock full of all the dirty things I'd like to whisper through any comms set-up when she shuts the truck door. She's halfway up the front steps before I've had time to get my mind out of my crotch. Or rather, hers.

Shoot, if I didn't know better, I'd think she was teasing me on purpose.

Six the following morning, and I arrive to find the lock-up's roller door open as far as it will go. I'm freaking out about all my tools having been stolen when I see Kelly moving about inside. Of her car, there's no sign.

Even dressed in disposable coveralls and wearing an industrial gasmask, I'd recognize her anywhere, with her curves imprinted on my psyche for eternity.

What I don't know is why she's here this early. The parade is still three days away. Despite falling behind because we were too busy exploring each other's bodies, we'll soon be back on schedule.

Unless she's here early because she wants to avoid me?

By the time I've climbed out of my truck, she's armed with a top-of-the-line spray gun, a compressor chugging away down the back of the lock-up. The paint and diesel fumes are bad enough to tell me this isn't her first coat.

Without a mask of my own, there isn't a chance I can stay inside, something that has me backing up and leaning against the front of my truck.

Rather than stop and join me, she keeps applying a top coat to the body of the float. Is it even worth my while waiting for her to finish? Without extractor fans or a mask, it'll be ages before I can breathe in there.

I've even grabbed my keys out of my pocket when the compressor splutters to a stop. Where did Kelly get it from? Because it's not mine.

I'm still wondering when she puts the spray head down on a large piece of cardboard, and walks out into the open, all while removing her mask. Yep, the red marks on her face tell me it's been more than a five-minute job.

After a curt nod in my direction, she walks around the side of the lock-up to where I now see she's parked her car, doubtless to avoid spray drift. After grabbing her phone, she makes a call that amounts to not much more than, "It's me. I've finished."

Only then does she give me her full attention.

"Sorry, I was hoping to have it done, and the place aired out before you got here." She then glances inside, as if assessing her handiwork. "I'd offer you the mask, but it's not mine."

I find out who it belongs to when a moment later, a guy in paint-splattered overalls walks around the far end of the row of lock-ups. He's huge. Not fat, huge. When he lumbers up next to us, how massive is plain to see.

The guy is a mountain, and I don't like the way he's ogling Kelly. Yet if I were to act on it as I want to, I'd get flattened.

And this jerk knows it. His smirk when he looks me in the eye says it all.

Hah, and women think they're the best communicators. There's no missing the guy's message. In summary, it says, "I like her. Back off."

It's therefore of some relief when Kelly is friendly toward 'Fridge', as the name on his overalls reads, and nothing more. After handing him back his gasmask, she waits while he puts it on and retrieves his spray gear.

And damn it if the guy doesn't exit carrying the compressor propped on one shoulder like it weighs nothing. Given the thing has wheels, it's obvious to me he's showboating, and why.

"Thanks for cleaning it for me, Fridge. We don't even have a sink in our unit."

"No worries, Kel. Any time. You just have to call me, you know that."

On hearing his shortening of her name, and the invitation to call, a jealousy that's spiked with anger, unfurls in my chest.

That's my woman he's talking to.

The realization that she's not and that I'd given up my rights by moving out, hits me hard. How could I have screwed it up? All I had to do was tell her I love her. How come it's so hard when you mean it?

One thing is for sure, and that is if I'm to win her back, whatever I do, it's gonna have to be as big a gesture as Fridge is tall. With no chance of me working in the lock-up this morning, I may as well head back to my folks' place.

I won't be idle though. I've got a new life to plan. And it's one that involves Kelly. I have to hope I haven't left it too late.

EIGHTEEN

KELLY

Despite stuffing the bag containing the costume in my walk-in closet when I got home the day before yesterday, I'm dying to have another peek. I want to see if I hadn't imagined how good it looked at the costume shop.

All too often I'd buy something and then, on arriving home, I'd find I no longer liked it. So many returns over the years. So many unworn outfits hanging at the back of the closet, their price tags still in place.

After peeling away the many layers of tape, I drag the costume from the bag and shake it out. I then lay it on the bed, the stretchy, thigh-high silver boots laying on the floor next to it.

I've never loved an outfit as much as I love this one.

Even better is when, after I try it on again, it once more passes the test. With proper make-up and liberal body shimmer it will be amazing. At least I hope so.

However, I won't know until the morning of the parade if it's enough to have Zac losing control again. Enough to make him say to me what I long to say to him.

The time will soon be right. I can feel it. Just as I feel Zac's attraction to me when we're working on the float down at the lock-up. It's there, in the way he looks at me when he thinks I'm busy.

My feelings for him have intensified as I've gotten to know the man beneath the mask. His explanations and aid are now friendly rather than seductive.

I doubt I'm alone in marveling at how things have changed between us, although I haven't lost my mind altogether. Given a moment's provocation, I'd still jump his bones.

However, some things are more important than a moment's satisfaction.

I'm up super early on the day of the parade. Not to continue working on the float, but working on myself. I want my skin to gleam and me looking as sexy in my real costume as Zac is in his.

I'm not giving anything away too soon though, and after checking everything for the umpteenth time, I then pull the second costume I'd hired over the top.

If you're going to surprise someone, then it has to be a big surprise, a spectacular surprise. A surprise that takes their breath away.

On the drive over to the lock-up garage, I'm nervous. My surprise will either go incredibly, or fail epically. Much as I want to hurry, I can't. The streets are already busy with people making their way to the parade route. The atmosphere is vibrant, the excitement contagious.

As I drive in the gates of the storage center, I see Zac is already there, hitching the float to his truck. He looks up, and after a moment's surprise, breaks into an evil grin.

It tells me he expected me to chicken out on riding the rocket with him. Hah, it's as if he doesn't know me at all.

After parking off to one side, I take a couple of calming breaths before I get out and lock the car. I've never been this nervous before, not even when making big presentations in my old job.

A final check of the Velcro tabs that secure the front of my fake outfit, and I'm as ready as I'll ever be. As I walk around the corner, the fabric of the hidden outfit rustles against my skin, adding to the thrill of what's coming.

"Morning, Kelly." While Zac's voice is full of warmth, there's no missing his disappointment when he gets an eyeful of my costume.

And to be honest, I can't blame him. I do rather resemble a baked potato. No doubt because that's what the Halloween costume is. He can't complain though, because it's silver as he'd asked for.

"Morning." I do my best to sound casual despite the butterflies that are busy doing somersaults in my tummy. They don't calm as we check everything on the float.

Zac's technical skills shine through as he double-checks every bolt and tie-down is tight. I can't help but admire his dedication and attention to detail, especially when checking the rocket.

We're riding that thing through the streets of Coogan's Break. The last thing either of us wants is a catastrophic failure that will see the rocket launching itself off the float for real.

We're working side-by-side, when I catch of flash of bright neon green out the corner of my eye. Hard to believe that in my nerves over my costume, I had given no thought to who'd drive Zac's truck.

On joining us, Clive holds his hand up in the Vulcan salute so beloved by Spock. "Live long and prosper. Sorry we're late."

Audrey, who's next to him and also dressed as a Martian, nods in agreement, the silver bobbles on her headband bouncing around. "All ready to go?"

I glance at Zac for confirmation, getting a double thumbs up.

Soon enough, Clive sits in the driver's seat of Zac's truck, with Audrey next to him, and Zac and me in the back. It's cramped, but safer than riding the float down to the start of the parade.

It was on settling in the back that I saw Zac and my helmets sitting in the middle of the bench seat. How could I have forgotten that part of my costume? I'd spent hours taming my crazy curls, and for nought.

Oh, that's right, too busy worrying about what Zac will think of what's underneath the baked potato. On the drive into town, Zac makes us both put our helmets on, carrying out tests to check they still work.

They work alright! It's as if Zac is whispering in my ear, leaving me hot enough that it's a good thing I'm foil-wrapped. Add some butter and call me done. I know he's feeling the same way when he slides his visor up and I see his face.

His gaze remains locked with mine longer than necessary, the electricity between us palpable. I can't wait to see his reaction when I reveal my surprise.

With the float in position, Zac climbs onto the rocket, straddling it and putting his feet on the plates he'd welded in place. The last thing he does is drape the Stars and Stripes around his shoulders.

Meanwhile, I stay where I am, waiting until right before the parade starts, with this arriving all too soon. A sharp tug on the Velcro tabs and the baked potato opens to reveal the stunning ensemble hidden beneath.

After stuffing the yards of silver foil in the back of the truck, I climb aboard the float. With his visor still in the UP position, I'm able to see Zac's eyes widen and his jaw drop in astonishment.

There's also no missing what he says under his breath. After bouncing around in my helmet, his dirty promise then heads straight for places it's no right to. Well, not when we're out in public.

It's at this point that I notice something I'd missed earlier, and that's the placement of the second set of footplates.

He wants me riding in front of him, rather than pillion? Ah, no way. My body isn't ready for that sort of contact. I motion for him to move forward, but he's not budging.

"Hell no, sweetheart," whispers Zac, his words clear in my helmet. "No way am I riding a rocket through the middle of Coogan's Break sporting a woody."

This image first tickles my brain, before working its way into my subconscious.

It's also something that has me giving thanks there are no kids on the float today. And not the first time I've thought this, either. Organizing the neighborhood kids would have been like herding cats.

Short of standing there arguing with him when the parade organizers are yelling for floats to get moving, I straddle the rocket in front of him. The moment my ass settles into his groin, I realize the parade will be both heaven and hell.

ZAC

I've expected a lot of things riding the rocket with Kelly, none of which has come to pass, although I'm about to.

Her ass jammed hard against my cock, my hands resting on her thighs, and I'm close to losing it. And I can tell by the way she's squirming that I'm not alone in my arousal.

I'm thinking it can't get worse when my foot taps the pedal that operates the gas struts and the front of the rocket jerks upward, before hissing back down.

"Oh, jeez." I risk taking one of my hands off Kelly's thighs to slide my visor down into place. Soon enough, I repeat the action with hers.

When my girl stiffens and forms a perfect 'O' in the middle of the Independence Day Parade, I want to be the only one to know what's happening. It's a thought that has me putting my hand back on her thigh, a little higher than before, and squeezing.

There's no missing her sharp intake of breath, with this audible through the helmet comms.

"Like that, do you?" I hit the gas strut pedal again. "Imagine if I was buried deep inside you right now?"

She gasps in response before adding, "Zac, don't."

Her words lack conviction, egging me on.

If I thought she was squirming before, it's nothing compared to now, with her ass working its magic on my cock. When Clive turns my truck onto Main Street, even my senses are overwhelmed.

While the continued rise and fall of the rocket has Kelly jammed hard up against me, the street is lined with people six-deep on either side. It's as if all eyes are on us. It's as if everyone knows.

"Oh, damn, baby. I hope you taped your nipples because I'll bet they're good and puckered."

It's not that I've ever considered an audience before, but the risk of being caught doing something bad adds a certain edge to proceedings. It's a thought that has me tapping the gas strut pedal twice in quick succession, being rewarded by Kelly moaning in my ear.

Hmmm, nope, I'm not alone. There's also never been a better time to tell her how I feel. I can deal with the fallout when the parade ends.

"Kelly, say nothing. Just hear me out, okay?"

Rather than answer, she jerks her head, the back of her helmet clunking against the visor of mine.

"I love you, Kelly. I can't imagine life without you. If the job in LA is that important to you, are you okay with me coming with you?"

In front of me, she stills. Other than her hand trembling when she throws candies to the kids in the crowd, it's as if I haven't spoken. As if I haven't handed her my heart for safekeeping.

Okay, so that's how it is. Her rejection cuts deep, with me doing my best to inch away from her. Anything to put some distance between us.

However, she's not done taunting me. She stretches her foot out and taps the gas strut pedal with her toe. This has the front of the rocket jerking upward again, although she does nothing to stay where she is.

She slides down the hull, her gorgeous ass jamming itself into my cock. "I turned the job down." I can tell by her labored breathing that we're still connected.

"Zac, I didn't know what we had, but I knew we had something. That we've got something." She falls silent, but for a second, before whispering, "I love you, too."

Because the speakers in the helmet are right next to my ears, I hear her quiet words. What I don't understand is why the crowd has erupted in wild cheering, with all eyes on us.

On hearing a squeal of feedback through a helmet designed to cope with outer space, I realize what's happened. "Oh, jeez."

Kelly's hiccup tells me when she catches on, too. All we can hope is that our innermost feelings only overrode the huge speakers out front of the local radio station at the moment we passed by, and not before.

Surely not before? A panicked check of the crowd shows no parents with hands slapped over their kids' ears to protect them from my dirty fantasies.

Much as I want to bury myself in Kelly's lush depths, I don't want the whole town knowing about it. And while delirious to know she loves me in return, I'm even happier to be wearing a full-face helmet.

It's times like these I wish we had pet names for each other. There was always a chance we could hide our true identities. With Coogan's Break as small as it is, by tomorrow morning, everyone will know who we are and what we said.

Rather than stopping at the end of the parade route, Clive keeps going, although he keeps his speed down. Even back at the lock-up, Kelly and I keep our thoughts to ourselves.

For all we know, Audrey and Clive might have heard

everything through the car radio. I've embarrassed myself and Kelly enough for one day.

We're still on the float when there are a couple of Martians next to it, dancing like there's no tomorrow.

On stepping down, Kelly and I are gathered up in a big hug. Clive and Audrey crowing that we've seen what everyone else could see, "As plain as day".

Such is my desire to park the trailer in the lock-up so I can park myself in Kelly, that it's only on my fourth attempt I manage it. Here's hoping I don't have the same issues later.

The drive to Sand 'O' Sun seems to take forever, with us having to crawl along to cope with the crowds of townspeople on their way home. Given the amount of cheering and knowing smiles, we might have been audible through those monster speakers for longer than we'd realized.

This has me thinking back to what I'd said to Kelly. Not to cringe, but so I can follow through on any promises I'd made. It's something that has me laughing out loud.

It's also something that has me making a mental note

to pick up an extra set of gas-struts. You never knew when they'd come in handy.

NINETEEN

KELLY

My hands shake as I grip the steering wheel. Not from nerves, but from excitement.

That I'll soon be able to show Zac, and tell him again, and again, that I love him, will be like winning gold at the Clio advertising awards.

On pulling to a stop in the driveway at home, and Zac parking next to me a second later, I decide it will be even better. The glint in his eye says I'm in for more fun than I ever had at any of those awards' dinners.

And all without shoehorning myself into a dress I hate, too. It's thinking about some horrors I've worn over the years that has me realizing something.

I'm still wearing my gorgeous alien costume. Focused as I have been on Zac's professions of love, I've been living inside my head ever since. I run my hands down the flowing skirts, the fabric silky to the touch.

Yep, better than any stupid awards dinner.

Zac stalks around the back of his truck, the space suit doing nothing to hide that he's as ready for me as I am for him. Walking backwards, I beckon him on, with him growling in response.

This has me squealing in delight before spinning and racing for the front steps. While it might seem as if I'm trying to escape, nothing could be further from the truth.

He catches up with me next to the front door, taking over putting the key in the lock, my trembling hands not up to the task. And anyway, I've got better things to do with my hands.

"You keep that up, sweetheart, and I'm gonna be taking you on the stairs."

I'm still deciding whether this would bother me when he opens the door, slamming it against the wall in his haste to get inside. There's no missing the crunch of the door handle hitting the drywall.

"Don't worry. I'll fix it."

He tosses my keys on the hall console, before slamming the front door with as much enthusiasm as he'd opened it. While the frosted glass panel rattles, it doesn't shatter. Meanwhile, I'm close to it.

A second later and my world is turned upside down when Zac bends and tosses me fireman-style over his shoulder. Him then putting his hand on my ass to steady me has him finding out that I'd opted for the gossamer French panties, after all.

There's nothing but a whisper of fabric between his hand and my derriere.

"Oh, my, God, woman. You'll be the death of me."

He's even taken a step toward my office when I yell at him. "Zac Thomas, the first time we make love for real will not be with me bent over my desk!"

He's grumbling about my being a spoilsport, when I laugh out, "We can do that later."

It's all the encouragement he needs, although I'm glad I hadn't bothered with breakfast when he races up the stairs.

I can't complain though, with his hand exploring my ass, and other places, on the way. Soon enough, he puts me down in the bedroom and I fall against him, my legs not up to supporting me.

It's a good thing they won't have to for much longer.

Zac slides his fingers inside the tops of the thigh-high boots that complete my outfit. Not content, he then runs his hands up the sides of my legs and under the skirts of my costume. When he slides them back down, he takes my sheer panties along for the ride.

I turn to allow him to unzip me, but he's got other ideas.

"No, my alien princess. I want you to keep everything else on. I've been dreaming of this ever since you ditched that hideous baked potato outfit." He then kisses the back of my neck in an act of reverence. "It's a shame we couldn't bring the rocket home."

I burst out laughing, both at his ridiculous notion, and because of the happiness bubbling up inside of me. Soon, that's not all that's inside of me. His hands snake down my front in a move designed to claim and arouse.

While I get to keep my costume on, Zac soon rids himself of his with impressive speed, standing in front of me, his smile alight in his eyes.

"Damn, but I love you, Kelly Sanderson." His hands on my upper arms, he pulls me tight against him, his lips searing mine in a kiss that's heated with love.

As hot as the sun beaming through the skylight above the bed, the silver of my costume casting light around the room. After wrapping my fingers tight around his length, I lock my gaze with his. "And I love you, Zac Thomas, but if I don't lie down, I'm going to fall down."

"Okay, let's get you off your feet."

After lifting me onto the end of the bed, Zac tips me back, leaving me half on and half off. However, he doesn't join me. Instead, he fluffs the front of my skirts up, exposing me to his gaze.

But he's not finished yet, nudging my knees to the sides. Rather than feeling vulnerable, I'm flooded with power.

To a backdrop of the reflections cast on the ceiling by my silver boots, he stands between my thighs, his cock soon nudging for permission. Finally, a plus to this bed being as tall as it is.

"Prepare to dock, Princess! I'm about to breach the final frontier."

There's nothing I can do not to giggle at his corny space jokes. However, I come close to choking on my laughter when he drives home with a single powerful thrust.

And I love every single inch of it, and him. As he withdraws and slams home again, and again, the pressure builds, my body coming alive as never. Soon enough, my muscles tighten in readiness.

All it takes to push me over the edge is for Zac's last few thrusts to be interspersed with him telling me, "I love you, Kelly, I love you."

I shatter, gasping out, "I love you too, Zac. I love you so much."

When he flops next to me and hugs me tight, I'm not sure why I'm close to tears, when I've never been happier in my life. While Zac had joked earlier that we were *docking*, I feel as though I'm home after years spent drifting through space and life.

ZAC

With Kelly hard up against me, my heart is ready to burst out of my chest like something out of Alien. I never realized love could be like this.

Instead of feeling tied down as I've always expected, I'm flooded with a euphoric contentment.

Funny that on Independence Day of all days, I'm happy to lose mine. And yet I've lost nothing. Quite the contrary.

With Kelly at my side, I can achieve anything. When she stares at me, her eyes brimming with love, I'm invincible. And, after the hell that asshole agency put her through, I hope to return the favor.

"I still can't believe you turned down Jason's job." My follow up kiss is one of gratitude. She chose me, and for that I'll be forever grateful.

While I'd been prepared to move to LA, I'm pleased I don't need to. Coogan's Break is part of who I am. "I thought it was what you wanted."

Next to me, Kelly stills, barely breathing, as if scared to speak.

"Come on, love. We just bared our souls to the whole blasted town."

Given how quickly we'd left the scene of our crime, we don't yet know how much of our conversation was overheard.

With any luck, it was only us declaring our love for each other. If the townsfolk overheard anything prior to that, we'll be getting disapproving looks for months to come.

"I thought I wanted the job, too. Then I realized it wouldn't keep me warm at night. It couldn't make me laugh. That as night follows day, there'd soon be another Jason."

She places her hand on my chest; her splayed fingers covering my heart. "I wanted more than that." She takes a deep breath before continuing. "Zac, I wanted you. I always will."

I'm bathing in the glory and listening to the angels sing, when she tweaks my nipple and bursts out laughing. "Come on, Zac. I want to ride the rocket again."

She doesn't need to ask twice with me more than willing to be taken by my alien princess.

Come dinner time, and we have, with each time better than the last. We've also had to ignore a heap of phone calls, and even someone hammering on the front door at one point.

After deciding the constant interruptions must be because our entire conversation had been overheard, we're happier staying where we are.

To us, the outside world has ceased to exist, at least until the fireworks start up, the loud whizzes and bangs the perfect soundtrack for our lovemaking.

Away from prying eyes and waggling tongues.

And speaking of waggling tongues...

I have Kelly flat on her back, her skirts hitched up, and am eating my fill a moment later. As I hum against her bud, my lips tingle, and she writhes and trembles at the mercy of my mouth.

"Oh Zac! Promise me you'll never learn the words to that song. Promise."

I break away, with her wailing in response. "So long as you tell the costume place that this outfit got ruined in the wash."

After pinging the tops of her stretchy boots to reinforce my wish, I go back to forgetting the words to the song she so loves.

It isn't until the following morning that we're ready to face the world, although even then it's wearing caps and dark glasses. We needn't have bothered. Coogan's Break was too small to hide for long.

Sure enough, we've grabbed takeaway coffees and are walking along the boardwalk when the cat calls start up. "Hey, Rocket Man!" Kelly is lucky in that she only gets referred to as Princess Leia twice.

"We can go hide if you like, but I reckon we should brazen our way out of it. We may as well get it over with."

Kelly doesn't appear convinced by my plan, so I instead go for a diversion.

"If you've turned down the LA job, what will you do?

What about the pet food place? Can't they give you some more work?"

As we continue along the boardwalk, Kelly tells me about an email she'd received from Caroline Burt, the owner of the pet food company.

"When she told me about the other company needing someone, I knew it would be enough to keep me going until I could get started."

I have to think about what she's said for a second. "Hang on? Get started? Get started on what?"

Kelly stops and looks at one of the many parking lots next to the beach. "You see that van over there, the one with the satellite dish on top?"

"Yeah. What of it?"

"Digital nomads." She then walks off, as though this has explained everything, rather than nothing.

"I'm gonna need more than that, Princess."

It turns out, unbeknownst to me, that every summer, Coogan's Break was home to scores of digital nomads. People who worked out the back of a van, sometimes for themselves, often for big corporates.

Just as Kelly's agency had done away with a couple of floors in a high rise, so had other companies. Why pay rent when you can have people working remotely? With a good internet connection, people could work from anywhere.

"That's not to say they don't want an office to work out of now and then. To access copiers, scanners, and the like. The kinda stuff you can't fit in the back of a van."

As we pass another parking lot, I see yet more vans. There's nothing low-tech about these tiny houses, with many tricked out with satellite dishes, air-con, the works.

Being a digital nomad must pay well.

"I can even offer them stuff like showers and a laundromat. The kinda thing that'll have them visiting, even in the winter. I was thinking of calling it The Oasis. Because, you know, where else would a digital nomad stay?"

It's obvious she's thought it through. The thing she hasn't covered is where she'll set up shop. "How much space do you need?"

She stops again, as if calculations and walking are mutually exclusive. "A couple of thousand feet, with plenty of parking. I've put the word out. But there's nothing suitable right now."

I don't speak, because the proposal I'm thinking of is a big step for both of us. It's also one that will involve one hell of a lot of work.

My having fallen silent, she turns to look at me. "Zac?"

"Okay, so here's the thing..."

The relief that Kelly is on board with my solution is immense. Much as I love staying with her at her family's vacation home, it doesn't feel right. I'm used to making my way in the world, not sponging off others, especially not the woman I love.

"Once we fix the house, we can move onto renovating the barn."

I say this like it's easy, when it'll be a huge undertaking. This is thanks to my plan to lift the house twelve feet in the air so it's not taken out by another flood.

The barn, being on higher ground, had been left untouched by the floodwaters, so converting it into office space and facilities should be straightforward enough.

That's if I can get the guys from work to help in their spare time.

On driving into my place with Kelly at my side, I'm nervous. She's the first woman I've ever brought here, so I hope she can see past the mess left behind by the flood.

Even after she's climbed out of my truck and looked up at the house, I'm unsure what she thinks of it all. However, I can tell by the way her eyes dart about that she's taking everything in.

Still without a word, she takes off down the bumpy gravel driveway before disappearing around the back of the house.

I find her with a hand up to shield her eyes from the sun. She's taking in the field and barn on the other side of hope creek. That she can see beyond the flood damage is clear by the wattage of her smile.

After I join her, she throws her arms around me and

squeezes tight, before reaching up on tiptoes and giving me a resounding kiss.

"Oh Zac, it'll be perfect!"

Okay, I hadn't expected this sort of enthusiasm, given the house sits in a sea of silt, with debris from homes further up the valley, strewn everywhere.

"It will be? I mean, do you think so?"

"Zac, with you at my side, of course, it will!"

Quick as a flash, I've scooped her up and am sloshing through the mud to the back door. Rather than stop, I boot the door in and cross the threshold with her in my arms.

There's nothing bridal about the moment. The place smells like a fetid swamp. And yet, with Kelly tight against my chest, I couldn't be happier.

EPILOGUE

ONE YEAR LATER

KELLY

As I take in the enormous float in the lean-to next to the barn that houses The Oasis, I have to marvel at the workmanship.

Zac and I could never have managed this on our own, but after we'd put a call out for help, we'd been inundated.

Thank goodness for the guys from Lucky Break helping with general construction. That and lots of the digital nomads staying at The Oasis for the summer have also pitched in. The van lifers, in particular, have a multitude of skills and a can-do attitude.

They also have a knack for creative solutions, with them often having to make-do and mend when on the road. I mean, who'd have thought you could create realistic palm trees from a stack of second-hand tires, with fronds hacked out of old carpets?

While I'm the one providing a haven for these nomads, I've learned so much from them in return. The other thing that's great is the buzz I get from being around other creative people.

It's an opportunity that's led to some award-winning collaborations. The night I'd collected a Gold Clio for one of my Burt's Pet Food campaigns will stay with me for a long time.

Beating Jason Ralph for the top spot had made all the hard work worth it. And of course, I'd held the gold statue high when I passed his table.

And it wasn't any old table Jason had been sitting at, but that reserved for top management, with Jason cozying up to Brian Mackey as though joined at the hip.

It had also shown me I'd been right to turn down the ECD job, with the patriarchy proving itself to be alive and well. It wasn't until after I'd said no I'd found out Jason was only back in Australia on vacation. A nasty sleight of hand by Brian Mackey, for sure.

If I'd gone back to LA, and that dream job, my life would have been hell, rather than the heaven that it is these days.

I watch Zac, who, with the help of Josh Kendrick, works on installing the red and purple canvas tent at the back of The Oasis Float.

A year on and I still have moments where I need to remind myself that Zac had chosen me. Other times, I can't imagine this gorgeous man not being a part of my life.

He is my wingman, although more often, he's my rocket man. I don't bother trying to hide my smile at the memories this brings back.

This will be the first time we've entered the Independence Day Parade in our own right. We're not doing so on a whim, though, with our goal from the very start being to win the top prize.

It was something we'd done with Mary's '*Out of this World*' float last year. Of course, we'd not found out about that until later, having done a runner after broadcasting our most intimate thoughts for all to hear.

However, it was because of the fun we'd had that we wanted to enter one of our own. No two-way communications though, with Zac still being called Rocket Man or Major Tom occasionally.

"Zac, I'll catch up with you later for something to eat."

His bark of laughter, and a groan from Josh, tells me I haven't been as subtle as I've thought. And I don't care, with that another thing Zac has taught me. These days I live for myself, not for others. Other than Zac, that is.

On entering the cool of the barn, the buzz is immediate, with people busy working away at the rows of hot desks. While most are wearing headphones and keeping to themselves, others sit in groups, discussing projects, or plain old gossiping.

Being an equal partner in the enterprise alongside Zac, I have an office of my own, which works out great, because my computer setup is far from portable. And as with my office at Sand 'O' Sun, this one also has a view.

Rather than looking out over Coogan's Break, my view is of the newest addition to The Oasis, a natural swimming pond. I'd always wanted one of these, and they were so much prettier than a normal swimming pool.

Zac loved them because they required less maintenance.

Either way, it's an inspiring view and I love watching the wildlife the pond attracts. Even better is when Zac cools off on a hot day. I'll never tire of his gorgeous body, never.

Just how balanced my life now is, is brought home when Zac knocks on my office door sometime later. "Sweetheart, I'm hungry."

"Oh, I didn't realize it was so late." A moment's confusion has me looking out the window. I've expected to see the shadows are longer, but they aren't. A check of the clock on my computer confirms it. "Oh, right, *that* sort of hungry."

After flicking off my computer, I stand and join him. Then, without a backward glance, I make a beeline for our bedroom over at the house.

Despite this, I'm not moving fast enough for Zac.

"Don't take too long. I might remember the words to that song you love so much."

To anyone overhearing our conversation, we could be taken as talking about our favorite tunes on Spotify. To me, it's enough to have my bud tingling in anticipation and me giggling, and breaking into a run.

Ten minutes later, and while Zac still can't remember the lyrics, I'm hitting the high notes of our special song.

ZAC

There's no dodging the flashbacks when Josh tows our float into position at the start of the parade. This year's costumes are so different from those we'd worn on the *Out of this World* float. This is both a good and bad thing.

Good for me because I'm way more comfortable. Bad because Kelly is also covered from head-to-toe in khaki. Neither of us were okay pretending to be Bedouin, opting instead to play the part of 1930s archeologists.

The moment Josh tows us into Main Street, the crowd recognizes us and the calls of Rocket Man start up, along with hooting and hollering. Having expected this, I hit the switch that starts the fountain in the middle of the float.

The tinkling water soon works its magic with the hooting and hollering, changing to ooohs and aaahs and delighted squeals from the scores of kids in the crowd.

"Wait until they see this." Kelly is grinning when she hits the big red button between us.

A moment later, something rises out of the sand that covers the front of the float. While the structure is fabricated from steel, the outside is canvas, painted to look like blocks.

When it reaches its zenith, it forms a perfect pyramid, one with a small Sphinx sitting atop it.

Next to me, Kelly is peering at it. "What's that? It wasn't there when I checked everything earlier."

Rather than answer, I laugh with delight that she's spotted it as quickly as she has. Kelly's all about the details. I've still not said anything when the pyramid subsides again, its components once again indistinguishable from the sand that surrounds it.

Determined to see what's on top of the pyramid, Kelly hits the red button again, pushing me off my cushion. "You're the archeologist. Go archeology the heck out of it."

Once on my feet, I tip my pith helmet in her direction before zig-zagging my way down the length of the float. I'm tall enough that I can reach out and grab the small statue before the pyramid again disappears.

Back next to her, I check where we are on the parade route, soon enough seeing my timing is perfect. Rather than sit, I drop to one knee in front of Kelly, her eyes widening in response.

"Kelly Sanderson, will you make my life complete by agreeing to marry me?" I then pop the top of the little sphinx, revealing the ring I'd picked up at the dollar store.

I've made my question clear and loud, hoping it will be picked up by the microphone I'd fitted to the brim of my pith helmet. The same sort of microphone I'd fitted to Kelly's helmet when I said I needed to tidy them up.

That the radio station public address system has picked up my question is confirmed when the DJ booms out, "Well, Kelly, are you going to say yes?"

She has to wait for the crowd to stop chanting SAY YES SAY YES SAY YES, before she can answer.

"Yes, I'll marry you, Zac Thomas. I'm happier with you than I've ever been in my life. I love you."

She then holds her hand out, allowing me to slip the makeshift ring onto her finger. With it in place, she rears up and throws her arms around my neck, in a move that has us collapsing back into the tent in a loving pile.

To a background of cheering, I reach up and release the flaps of the tent and they drop shut, sealing us in our own little world. Although not completely, with us able to hear the calls of "Go for it, Rocket Man" from the more raucous members of the crowd.

On deepening our kiss, I realize that once again we're going to miss the end of the parade. I then grab our pith helmets and toss them through the flaps of the tent, because there are some things that I don't want the crowd to hear.

That done, I collect my phone from the pocket of my safari jacket. "Josh, mate, don't stop, not until we're back at The Oasis." I end the call, not giving him a chance to respond.

After ditching my phone, I wrap my arms around Kelly, kissing her. "You know the gas struts in the pyramid?"

"Hmmm, yes." Her response is distracted with her busy sliding her leg between mine and nudging me where it counts.

"Well, today, sweetheart, is your lucky day, because they weren't the only gas struts I fitted on this thing."

"Oooh Zac Thomas, you are a wicked man. But you're wrong. My lucky day was the day I met you."

She then deepens our kiss and I know that from here on in, all our days will be lucky, not just today.

THANK YOU

If you've enjoyed this story, we'd be thrilled if you could take the time to give it a rating, or even a review, before you leave. In the meantime, carry on to read more about what's coming up next.

Many thanks
The Birds at Bad Birds

BAD BIRDS

Bad Birds is a branch (some say twig)
of Squabbling Sparrows Press

ALL ABOUT HOPE

Hope believes everyone deserves love, especially curvy girls. She also likes to believe there's a welcoming town like Coogan's Break for all of us. A place where the girls are curvy and the guys hotter than hell, where opposites attract, and love is steamy and fast.

www.sparrows.online

Meet the **Lucky Break Construction** crew, whose motto should read ***"If we build it, you will come!"*** because apparently a few Coogan's Break single ladies have done just that.

Available from all good online retailers.

If you've enjoyed your time in Coogan's Break, consider staying a while, by treating yourself to the large format six packs of books 1-6 and 7-12. Available from all good online retailers.

CONTENT WARNING:
SNARKY, RAUNCHY, BRITISH ENGLISH!

Journey back to the wild late seventies with The Seventies Collective—a rollicking adventure through an era defined by its outrageous language, even more outrageous behaviour, and hairstyles that defied gravity.

The humour is a glorious fusion of Australasian and British wit—sharp, satirical, and that can be unapologetically in-your-face in places. If you're easily offended, this is NOT the series for you.

Available from all good online retailers.

MARINA WITCHES
COZY MYSTERY SERIES

ANDIE LOW

Frankie's a jinxed witch with Bruce Lee moves.
Dex is her snarky Jack Russell. Together with Zane,
Frankie's drop-dead gorgeous, neighbor,
these three are magic.

Left in charge of her grandmother's marriage agency, vampire matchmaker, Eva De Silva, is expecting a peaceful gig. She's wrong.

On her first night, she's hit with unexpected visitors, a dangerous family relic goes missing, and she's framed for murder. Luckily, she has Dominik Zilonka—her newest client and vampire voted least likely to settle down—on hand to help.

Eva must stay sharp to save the business, clear her name, and find Dominik a wife, all while ignoring that she's his perfect blood bond.

Dead and Married - Trade and Large Print Paperbacks available from all good online retailers. Can also be ordered in by your local library.